Janie Bolitho was born in Falmouth, Cornwall. She enjoyed a variety of careers – psychiatric nurse, debt collector, working for a tour operator, a book-maker's clerk – before becoming a full-time writer. She passed away in 2002.

PLOTTED IN CORNWALL

JANIE BOLITHO

Allison & Busby Limited
12 Fitzroy Mews
London W1T 6DW
allisonandbusby.com

First published in Great Britain in 2001.
This paperback edition published by Allison & Busby in 2015.

A CIP catalogue record for this book is available from
the British Library.

10 9 8 7 6 5 4 3 2 1

ISBN 978-0-7490-1799-6

Typeset in 10.5/15.5 pt Sabon by
Allison & Busby Ltd.

The paper used for this Allison & Busby publication
has been produced from trees that have been legally sourced
from well-managed and credibly certified forests.

Printed and bound by
CPI Group (UK) Ltd, Croydon, CR0 4YY

For Teresa Chris, my agent and my friend

CHAPTER ONE

It might have been a Tuesday morning in mid-November but the traffic on the A30 heading up the county was slow-moving. No caravans and camper vans now, the holiday season was over. But in the distance, seen easily on the long, straight stretch of road, was a tractor towing an empty, mud-splattered trailer. That, in conjunction with the incessant rain which was impairing visibility, was delaying the vehicles ahead. No dual carriageway here, no way of passing, a case of being patient until the farm vehicle turned off or found somewhere to pull in.

She wound the window down an inch or so. On either side of her the countryside was flat. Nothing but bracken, brown and rain-sodden, so very different from the picturesque coves and golden beaches of the coastline. Ahead lay Bodmin Moor, Rose Trevelyan's destination. She had memorised the directions given to her over the telephone by Louisa Jordan. There were, she had told Rose, no signposts, merely a track which led to the house.

The wipers swept sheets of water across the windscreen

as the sky darkened and the rain fell more heavily. It was a dismal, foreboding sort of day but not to Rose who was looking forward to meeting the two sisters and discovering their exact requirements. 'If you reach Jamaica Inn you've gone too far,' Mrs Jordan had told her in a pleasant, well-modulated voice.

The tractor turned into a farm gateway depositing dollops of mud from the trailer wheels in its wake. The smell of manure hung in the air. In a nearby field sheep bleated plaintively. The cars in front speeded up, Rose followed suit. Bisland was signposted. 'Go past that turn-off,' she had been instructed. 'About two miles on there's another left turn, ignore that one also, then take the very next left.' The track leading off the main road appeared as no more than a small gap in the straggling winter foliage. Rose indicated and swung on to it, the suspension protesting as the car lurched over the potholes. There was nothing to indicate a dwelling, no house name carved on a piece of wood at the entrance to the track, no clue at all that anyone lived there. Sisters, not young by the sound of Louisa's voice, but voices were deceptive over the telephone. Recluses, maybe? Soon she would know.

Very slowly she followed the track for a mile and a half. Ahead she saw a house, first its chimneys and roof, then the rest of it came into view. The landscape seemed flat but could not have been or the building would have been visible from the road. It was a typical Cornish farmhouse, built of granite, except there were no outbuildings. It was almost square, two-storeyed, with four windows set equidistant from the solid wooden door.

The track simply ended. There was no garden in front of

the house, the moors closed in, surrounding it, claiming it for their own. Glad of her leather boots, Rose got out of the car and sloshed through the puddles. No lights shone behind those windows and the smoke which arose from the chimneys was obscured by the rain. But Rose could smell the pungency of wood-smoke. She wondered if she had made a mistake, had come on the wrong day, despite the Rover parked at the side of the house. But seconds after she had rapped the heavy iron knocker against the solid wooden door it was opened.

'Mrs Trevelyan, how lovely to meet you. Do come in. I'm Louisa. We weren't sure you'd make it on such an awful day.'

Rose stepped inside and wiped her feet on the rough doormat. The flagstone passage ran the length of the building, straight to the back door, the top half of which was of dimpled glass surrounded by panels of stained glass. Doors opened off both sides of the passageway, a staircase ascended on the left-hand side. The banisters were substantial, ornately carved and probably original. Rose was shown into a room at the back on the right.

'My sister, Wendy,' Louisa Jordan said, nodding towards a smaller, older woman who sat by a fire which roared up the chimney. Its flames cast shadows over the maple furniture which glowed like the syrup from the sugar of the tree.

'Hello, I'm Rose Trevelyan.'

Wendy stood up and shook her hand. Her skin was smooth but her grip was firm. She was not as old as her hunched pose had suggested and when she smiled it was easy to see she had been attractive in her youth. 'We've laid a tray. I'll fetch the coffee while you get yourself warm. Sit by the fire, my dear.'

Rose did so, sinking into the deep velvet cushion of the armchair. She had come a long way with no certainty of getting the commission. This visit was to discuss the possibility and arrange terms if anything came of it. These women, for whatever reasons, wanted a portrait painted, one of them both together. Two for the price of one? Rose wondered. Within those first few minutes she had been studying her possible clients and their surroundings, her artist's eye taking everything in quickly, gaining impressions, feeling her way. Wendy was small-boned but sturdy, smartly dressed in a plain brown skirt with a split at the back. Her cream sweater was appliqued and looked soft and expensive. She was sensibly shod and her greying hair was cut short. Yes, smart, but somehow ordinary now, the smile the only evidence of faded beauty. Her face would be easier to photograph than to paint.

Louisa was altogether different. She was still beautiful. A London cocktail bar would have been a more appropriate setting than a bleak house in the middle of Bodmin Moor. Her pale hair was completely straight, cut expertly from a side parting to fall in two points to just below her ears. Her lilac wool dress and jacket might be simple but had been designed to show off her figure. Wendy was about sixty, Rose decided, Louisa almost certainly a decade younger, possibly even more. Not farmers, nor from farming families, hard work had not touched their lives, but Cornish even if the accent was imperceptible, the vowels only drawn out fractionally. So what were these elegant women doing in the middle of nowhere when they so obviously enjoyed the good things in life?

'Let me take your coat if you're warm enough,' Louisa

said, moving towards her on soft leather court shoes.

'Thank you. That fire throws out a lot of heat.' Rose handed her the three-quarter length tan wool jacket.

Louisa took it and draped it carefully over the back of a chair. 'We've had to get used to making it do so. We have no gas or electricity here. Fortunately we do have running water. The electricity people are only prepared to link us up to the National Grid if we're prepared to part with thirty-seven thousand pounds. Don't look so surprised, Mrs Trevelyan,' she said as she sank into the depths of the apricot-coloured settee which matched Rose's chair. 'We're by no means the only ones in deeply rural areas in the same position. However, we have open fires in all the rooms, plenty of hot water, and the most reliable Cornish range which provides not only the hot water but heat in the kitchen and our cooking facilities. And these.' She waved an arm to indicate the pretty glass-shaded oil lamps scattered around the room. 'It's rather fun, actually, and it means our privacy is not invaded by the hideousness of television. However,' she smiled at the astonishment on Rose's face, 'we're not totally cut off from so-called civilisation, we have a battery-powered radio, and the telephone.

'We're a bit all or nothing these days. We had the option of our own generator but we decided that as five previous generations had managed without one, so would we.'

Not reclusive, Rose decided, because the clothes and haircuts said otherwise. There would be regular trips into Bodmin, or, more likely, Plymouth or Exeter for shopping. Not reclusive but quite possibly eccentric. Rose's curiosity was aroused. And, as her friends told her often enough, she possessed more than a fair share of that.

And what a house. How different the inside from the dour impression of the exterior, even allowing for the influence of the weather. Her feet had sunk into the thick carpet of a colour even Rose found hard to describe, except that it toned with the settee and armchairs. Not apricot, but the apricot side of brown. Tall glass doors with leaded panes stood at the back of the room leading out to an area of patchy grass, beyond which the moors stretched into the distance, the horizon invisible, merged with low cloud and blurred by the rain. The furniture was obviously cared for as much as the women cared for themselves. It was a room in which Rose felt comfortable, one which was bright and cheerful and managed to diminish the gloom outside. But it crossed her mind briefly that these women, as a matter of pride, may have dressed up for her benefit and that this might be the only inhabitable room in the place. She had been in similar situations before, where poverty was shamefully disguised. Could they really afford her services?

Wendy returned with the coffee. If this was a facade to impress, it was a good one. The tray was silver, the flowered cups and saucers were crafted from delicate bone china and the biscuits were thin, covered with rich dark chocolate, Belgian or Swiss, not the sort that could be purchased in village stores. She could smell the bitterness of good strong ground coffee. Mercenary bitch, Rose thought as she calculated that if all their possessions were such, they could certainly afford to pay her travelling expenses and the fee she had decided upon. If they offered her the commission, of course.

It was time to get down to business. 'What did you have

in mind, Mrs Jordan?' It was Louisa, the younger woman, to whom Rose addressed the question. In households comprising of more than one person there was often a demarcation of roles. Wendy had made the coffee and therefore might be the more subservient. But it was too soon to judge, and it was her sister who stood to pour the coffee.

'Sugar? Cream?' Louisa Jordan said as she gave the question some thought.

'Neither, thank you. Just black.' Rose picked up the cup by its intricate handle and took a sip. The coffee was excellent. She felt quite relaxed, warm and comfortable as she breathed in the scent of apple wood from the fire.

'Head and shoulders,' Louisa said once she had sat down, her own coffee in front of her. 'It's more striking than full-length don't you think?'

'Yes.' But more difficult, too, Rose thought with momentary panic. Full-length portraits could convey the essence of a person without the total accuracy required of enlarged facial features. A way of standing, a certain way of holding the head or a familiar gesture captured by the artist were often more telling than the precise position of a mole. Louisa Jordan had a strong, handsome face. Whoever painted the sisters together, regardless of how they chose to pose them and no matter what their technique, Rose was certain that the younger one would still appear dominant. 'May I ask why you want me to paint you?'

'You in particular, or why we decided to have it done?'

'The latter.'

'Does it matter?' Wendy, her cup halfway to her mouth, looked over it with an expression of surprise.

13

'Yes, in a way. You see, if it's just for yourselves, for fun, if you like, I would pose you differently from the way I would if the painting were to be hung alongside other family portraits. You see, even with a head and shoulders there are levels of formality and the question of whether you want full face or profile.'

Louisa laughed. 'I think we were right in our choice of artist, Wendy.' She turned to Rose. 'We very much admire your work, Mrs Trevelyan. We have one of your seascapes in the dining-room. When could you start?'

'But we haven't discussed the cost yet.' Rose was shocked. She was new to this. Normally her paintings were hung in galleries or local shops with a price sticker already attached. They either sold or they didn't but she rarely met the buyer. Her photography rates were fixed, a price list available to anyone who was interested. Negotiating payment was embarrassing.

'Oh, we have a rough idea of the going rate. We're prepared to add another one hundred pounds on top of it and, naturally, we'll pay all your travelling expenses.'

Rose placed her empty cup on the table beside her. They were obviously expecting great things. Was she good enough? There's only one way to find out, she decided as she looked up and smiled. 'Thank you. I could start next week. Thursdays suit me best. I'll need to make some preliminary sketches first, and possibly take some photographs. Not to work from, you understand, I never do that, just to capture various expressions. I like to study my subjects before I begin.

'You didn't say, what made you decide to commission someone?'

Louisa glanced at Wendy, indicating she should reply. 'It's just for us, a whim if you like, a bit of fun, as you put it. There are no family portraits. I have never married, and Louisa's husband left her. There's no one who'll be interested after we're dead. More coffee, Mrs Trevelyan?'

Rose accepted. A few more minutes of her time wouldn't hurt, especially now she saw she might have been wrong about the dynamics. It was essential to know something of the people she was to paint before she could capture them accurately in oils, but more interesting was the fact that there was something going on she did not understand, some undercurrent between the two women. Wendy had given her some basic information but the abrupt ending of her speech implied that that was all that she would be getting. Surely vanity was not the only reason they had engaged her?

When she left, Rose was in possession of a cheque for a hundred pounds as an advance towards petrol but with no idea why the portrait seemed important to her clients.

Driving back through the murky late morning she decided it didn't matter; it was work, therefore it was money and, more importantly, it was recognition. And she was excited at this new opportunity. Only recently had she branched out into portraits, and with more success than she had anticipated. She couldn't wait to tell Laura and Barry Rowe and, of course, her parents.

The journey was uneventful and she settled into it. Leaving the moors behind she wound through more lush countryside. There were trees and small rivers, full now, running beneath them. Then came the bleakness of tin-mining areas, disused engine houses and mine stacks crumbled in their surroundings of boulders and scrub-land and gorse, the only testament to a once thriving industry. But she smiled as she always did, as everyone from West Cornwall did when the road began to dip towards the sea, or the train they were on emerged from Marazion marshes, and St Michael's Mount could be seen rising out of the bay. She was home.

There were fields now, some green, the grass fattened by the rain, others brown, ploughed, where the daffodils grew, the bulbs already planted. The buds would be picked in January, earlier than elsewhere because of the temperate climate, then sold in shops throughout the country. For the locals there were often daffodils at Christmas. The sea lay ahead. It was never grey not even on such a day but full of colours which changed with the light which many artists had tried to capture over the decades. Some had been successful. Rose was one of them. She reached the outskirts of Penzance and headed towards the town centre before taking the road along the seafront which led to Newlyn and home. Her home for thirty years. But would it have been so if she had not married David who was a Cornishman? So many people wanted to share this different way of life – the slowness, the intimacy, the lack of worldliness which was a throwback in time – yet few truly adjusted and some were never accepted. Too many wanted all this and more, they wanted to incorporate all the things they were supposedly getting away from.

The wide sweep of the bay was to her left. The rain had eased, only a light drizzle dotted the windscreen. On the horizon a band of yellow light pushed the greyness upwards, which meant inland, taking the rain to other parts of the country. Rose had learnt the signs. Ask a fisherman, she thought, ask a farmer or anyone else whose livelihood depends on the weather and they'll give you a far more accurate forecast than any meteorologist sitting in front of a computer in Bristol. Those that are left, she thought sadly, hoping that Laura's husband, Trevor, would never have to decommission his trawler because he knew no other life than the one he had learnt from his father and grandfather. But Cornwall isn't yet the giant theme-park the government wants it to become while the Spanish trawl British waters and French farmers supply our shops and supermarkets, while fishermen's families starve and the last farmer declares himself bankrupt or commits suicide, Rose thought angrily, echoing what many others also thought. For that's the way things are going. She was angry with herself, too, because she had no way of stopping it.

She crossed Newlyn Bridge and turned left, passing the fish market, now closed for the day, all business concluded by the middle of the morning, then continued on up the hill.

Home, she thought, pleased to be there. She swung the car into the steep drive at the side of the house and parked at the top of it. There were things to do: a picture to frame, one roll of film to develop up in the attic which doubled as a studio and darkroom but was used far less lately. Most of her work was done outdoors.

Rose shook the kettle, decided there was enough water in it and plugged it in. Whilst it boiled she checked the answering-machine next to the telephone which stood on a table behind the living-room door. There were no messages. Arms folded, she looked out from her high vantage point over Mount's Bay. It had stopped raining and a watery sun had turned the sea silver. I was right about the weather, she thought with satisfaction as she heard the click of the automatic kettle switching itself off.

She recrossed the narrow hallway and made tea, sitting at the kitchen table to drink it. She wasn't hungry, she was too excited to eat, but she rarely ate much in the day. Her evening meal was something she always looked forward to. A glass of wine first, of course, and several with it. Louisa and Wendy, Wendy and Louisa. 'I don't know what to make of them,' she muttered as she reached for her handbag and removed the cheque. Not a joint bank account, then. The name printed on it and the signature belonged to Louisa Jordan. Perhaps the house and contents were hers and she had taken in her unmarried sister when the husband left her.

'Leave it, Rose, it's none of your business,' she could hear Barry Rowe telling her with that funny frown and his perpetual habit of pushing his glasses up the bridge of his nose with his forefinger. Well, maybe she would find out and maybe she wouldn't. Carrying her refilled mug of steaming tea across the flagstone hallway she dialled Laura Penrose's number, unable to wait to tell her the news. And then, she decided, she ought to do those chores and some paperwork and, if she felt really virtuous, the ironing . . .

Rose grinned as she put down the phone. There wouldn't be time for the ironing. Trevor had gone to sea that morning so Laura had invited herself over for supper. 'I'd better come round and help you celebrate. I'll bring the necessary liquid refreshment,' she had told Rose. 'You can dig out some of the fish you're stockpiling even though I'm sick of it myself.'

Which meant, Rose knew, making more of an effort than usual. But Laura was worth it. Laura was her friend,

18

and had been since they were young women. They had survived so much together: Laura's marriage and the births of her three sons and, in turn, their own marriages and the births of grandchildren; and Rose's marriage and David's death. But no Trevelyan children. It had never happened and by the time David became ill Rose had no longer cared. She was glad that there had been no distractions, nothing to take her attention away from him, especially at the end. They had been lucky in that they understood one another but allowed each other space. Yet how different we were, she thought. David was a big man in body and heart, a tidy precise man, a mining engineer, in the days when mines still existed in Cornwall. Rose was untidy, happy to live life in a muddle, rarely bothering to dress up. 'The eternal art student,' David had once called her, but not minding.

But she had dressed up that morning: gypsy skirt, feminine blouse, short, tight-fitting black jacket and long boots. Prospective clients would not have been impressed with her usual attire. Laura would be surprised to see her thus dressed and not in jeans. Laura, who it was hard to believe was out of her thirties, let alone a grandmother. But they had both worn well, she realised as she opened the freezer door. The fish would thaw in no time. She forgot the invoices waiting to be sent out and started preparing a lime and basil marinade for the plaice and a spicy sauce for the prawns.

CHAPTER TWO

Joel Penhaligon enjoyed the weekly art classes. There he could live for the moment, his brain, eyes and hand working in coordination, everything else forgotten. He also enjoyed walking, being buffeted by the wind, so he should have been happy as he made his way from the bus station over Ross Bridge and along by Penzance harbour on Wednesday evening. Fewer craft were moored there now that it was winter. *Scillion III* had stopped her daily crossings to and from the Scilly Isles a fortnight ago. Only the blue hulk of the *Gri Marita* ran now, carrying food and supplies to the islanders, and the occasional passenger who could stomach the rolling swell where five channels of water met once the coastline was left behind.

But Joel was troubled. His mother knew it but said nothing. He was aware of her love for him, but his father always came first. Joel wondered why this should be when the man was a bully.

'I'm firm but fair,' Roger Penhaligon was fond of saying. But Joel did not think he was being fair to his son.

Roger had married Petra when he was almost thirty and she only nineteen. Joel suspected he had needed a younger woman, one whom he could mould. He was their only child. Or maybe I'm just cynical, he thought as, hands in the pockets of his leather jacket, his canvas bag slung over his shoulder, he trudged up the deserted narrow cobbled lane behind the Dolphin Inn. He turned right and carried on up a steeper hill to where the classes were held.

'I must have it out with him, make my intentions clear and face the consequences,' he muttered, his words carried away by the freshening wind.

As he reached the studio he had an idea. He would enlist the help of the one person who had faith in him. And he would ask her that night. Joel stepped into the comparative warmth of the barn-like room. It was the annexe to a gallery but worlds apart from the building next door. The gallery had polished wood floors and was all white and chrome. There were plate-glass windows and cleverly concealed lighting. The current exhibition by a Mousehole artist was of modern art. The walls were adorned with vibrant swirls of colour on canvas while the small alcoves housed work by other local artists, including Rose Trevelyan.

But in the studio the sash windows, set high in the wall, rattled and the hollow sound of the wind reverberated behind the bricked-up fireplace. Ancient cast-iron radiators, thick with layers of institutional cream paint, gurgled and provided what warmth there was, but not enough to combat the draught which swept across the floor with each strengthening gust of the predicted Force 8. There was no dampness, no sign of the previous day's rain. The wind had dried the roads and pavements by morning.

November, the onset of winter, Joel's favourite season. It would bring storms to the coast and ships to the sanctuary of the wide arms of the bay. The class began; Joel settled down to work.

His tutor walked slowly behind the semicircle of chairs in which eleven other people sat, their heads bent in concentration. 'That's good, Joel,' she said, leaning over his shoulder. And he knew that it was and that she had meant it. He inclined his head in acknowledgement of the praise and carried on drawing.

'Can you spare a minute?' he asked when the two-hour class was over.

'Of course.'

Joel explained his predicament and wondered if he sounded as immature and sullen to the woman in front of him as he did to himself. At least she was listening.

'Yes. If you think it'll help, I'll do it,' she said, surprising him by her ready agreement.

Joel's step was much lighter as he made his way back to the bus station. He began the journey home in the brightly lit bus. Once they'd left Penzance only darkness surrounded them. The bus's headlights picked out hedges and fields as it wound its way towards St Just. Before it reached its destination Joel alighted on the main road and walked down a narrower road to where he lived. The imprint of the red tail-lights remained on his retinas for several seconds.

The gate was open and lights blazed from the house. The evergreen shrubs in the front garden swayed wildly and the weathervane creaked on the rooftop. He let himself in. The house was warm and smelt of polish which Petra Penhaligon's cleaning lady used to excess. Wednesday was one of her days.

'Is that you, Joel?'

'Yes.'

'I'm in the kitchen.' Petra smiled at her son. 'Are you hungry? I've saved you some chicken casserole.'

'I am. Thanks.' He took off his jacket and hung it over the back of a stool then sat at the breakfast bar in the large kitchen. 'Where's Dad?'

'At a meeting.'

Joel sighed. He should have guessed. His father owned a chain of caravan sites all supervised by managers. He rarely needed to visit them so had volunteered his services to many committees and filled his time by serving on them. 'I wanted to speak to him.'

'What about?'

Joel pushed back his dark hair. 'About my future.'

Petra Penhaligon folded her arms and pursed her lips. She had once been fragile and fair but, like many attractive blondes, with the passing of youth her looks and colouring had taken on a faded quality. Without make-up she seemed washed out, anonymous. 'There's plenty of time for that. You've got almost another year at school yet.'

I'm wasting my breath, Joel thought. Whatever I say she'll agree with my father.

A car crunched over the gravel and headlights swept across the kitchen ceiling. Petra's face lit up. The front door opened and closed and Roger Penhaligon came into the kitchen bringing with him some of the chill from outside.

23

'How did the meeting go?' she asked as she spooned a large helping of chicken and vegetables into a dish for Joel.

'Oh, you know how it is. A load of old women, some of them.' He smelt of whisky and cigars. He was a big man, over six feet and heavy from good living. The buttons strained across the waistcoat he wore under his suit jacket.

They're rich, Joel thought, rich enough that they could help me, but they won't, not unless I conform to their plans for me. He didn't want to be a doctor or a lawyer, nor did he want to take over his father's business, he wanted to paint. That was all he had ever wanted.

'What? Art college?' his father had said scornfully, even though he was smiling, when Joel had first mentioned it. 'Are you telling me your happiness lies in hanging around with a load of scruffy hippies?'

The comment was typical of his father's attitude. A staunch right-winger and a bigot, that's what he is, Joel had thought, and still did, not understanding him.

'It's what I want to do.'

'Plenty of time to decide, Joel. Let's not rush things.'

That had been a year ago but his mother had said the same thing tonight. Each time he mentioned it the response was evasive or along the lines that he'd never be able to afford to keep himself.

He looked at his father's implacable face as he sat at the farmhouse table at the other end of the kitchen and read his mood. There would be no discussion that night, Joel's views would not be countenanced.

Roger Penhaligon's skin was flushed and his jowls

quivered as he gave Petra a brief outline of what had taken place that evening.

I don't understand it, he didn't make any fuss about the evening classes, he even paid for them, Joel thought. Maybe he hoped they would get the idea out of my system. But they had only made him more determined to persevere. 'I'd like you to meet someone,' Joel said abruptly

'What, now?' Roger looked around the kitchen as though there might be a person in their presence he had not noticed.

'No. Soon.' Don't let me down, he prayed. He rarely spoke to his tutor, except about his work, but there was something about her which suggested she would help if she could.

'A girl?' Roger grinned. That was an interest he could understand.

'A woman, actually. I'll let you know when I've made the arrangements. I wanted to make sure you'd both be here. How about Friday, around five?' Head averted, he was still aware of the glance exchanged between his parents. Let them wonder, let them think what they liked. One day he would show them. One day they might even be proud of him.

'Suits me,' Roger said with a shrug of bafflement.

'Good. Thanks. I think I'll go up now.' He put his plate in the dishwasher and said goodnight. He was tired, pleasantly so, and his stomach was full. He knew he would sleep soundly. There was the clink of a bottle on glass as he left the room. Whisky for his father.

His mother's cat, a long-haired pedigree, sat on the second from bottom stair washing itself. As Joel passed it it hissed. He ignored it; the dislike was mutual. Upstairs he walked to his bedroom at the end of the gallery. It was large, as were all the rooms in the house which had once belonged to a high-ranking naval officer with five children. The place was an extravagance for three of them but at least it ensured privacy. His parents enjoyed entertaining but Joel never invited anyone back. His mother would fuss and his father embarrassed him, although he didn't know why.

In bed he studied what he had drawn earlier that evening, holding the sketchpad at arm's length. They had been working on figures, the human form. He had drawn a seated girl, her hands clasped around drawn-up knees, her head on one side. It was good. It was Miranda. He had drawn her from memory. He smiled. His poor tutor. He had seen the efforts of two of his fellow classmates and knew she was wasting her time with them. 'It doesn't really matter, though,' he said aloud. 'They're enjoying themselves anyway.'

Reaching out he switched off the bedside light and lay down beneath the warmth of the duvet, his hands cupped behind his head. The room was in total darkness. There was no moon, and no streetlights that far out in the country. Joel liked the dark, it enabled him to think. And think he must if his parents weren't going to finance his future studies. There were student loans, of course, and he could always get a part-time job. He listened to the wind as it moaned through the trees and the familiar, sometimes irritating tap of a branch on the window.

It was at such times that he missed Miranda, his cousin

who had been more like a sister. It was over a year since she had disappeared and no one had heard from her since. It hurt Joel that she had not contacted him, that there hadn't been a single telephone call or postcard to say that she was well and happy. Had Miranda still been around she would have stood up for him, faced down his father and told him where he was going wrong. Miranda feared no one. Well, he had to rely on someone else now. She'll come, he reassured himself. She's the sort of person who keeps her word. But that didn't necessarily mean she'd have any success.

'I liked her,' Louisa said as she began to clear the dining-room table on Wednesday evening. Her movements created a draught. The flame of the oil lamps flickered behind their yellow glass globes and made her shadow dance on the wall.

Wendy sipped the last of her wine and got up to help. 'Mm, so did I. Do you think she'll do a good job?'

Louisa shrugged as they carried the dishes through to the kitchen. They washed up themselves, there was more than enough for their cleaning woman to do. Louisa filled the sink and dropped in the cutlery. 'We can only go by her other work. There's something powerful about her scenery. She really knows how to capture it. However, we agreed we wanted an unknown in the portrait world. It would be wonderful if we were one of the first to commission her and she becomes recognised. Besides . . .' she stopped, and began to scrub a plate vigorously.

'I know,' Wendy said, touching her arm. 'I know, Louisa, but we have to try not to think about it. We've made a new start here.'

'It hasn't stopped the memories, though. It's hard, you know. There isn't a minute when I don't wish I could turn back the clock and make things have happened differently.'

'You're not to blame. The situation should never have been tolerated for so long. Be patient, give it another year and maybe you'll realise that this was all for the best.' Wendy picked up the warm, dry tea-towel which had been hanging over the brass rail along the front of the Cornish range. Starting anew, getting used to the inconvenience of no electricity had been a way of putting the past behind them, especially for Louisa. But they had adapted and now they were settled and comfortable there was little to divert them except for shopping trips and the odd morning at the hairdresser's. They were resourceful women, they had hobbies and they both read, but Wendy knew that Louisa still had the nights to endure, nights like this when the wind swept over the moors as if it sought revenge, when only the gnarled gorse with its spiky thorns stood up to it. Yet it had been a hot summer's day when Louisa's life had changed and, because of what followed, so had Wendy's.

Wendy went from room to room checking that the windows were secure and the fires safely damped down. A local farmer delivered logs, a sideline of his, and the coal merchant came once a month. Kindling they gathered themselves, from the moors, which provided little, and from country walks when they drove to wooded areas and filled plastic sacks with sticks and small branches. Wendy smiled wryly. The endless quest for kindling had become almost an obsession. But it gave them exercise and the bending was good for her stiff hip.

Louisa wiped every surface clean, rinsed out the dishcloth and hung it over the tap. The previous occupants had been responsible for the installation of running water. Without it she would never have considered the purchase. She sighed. There was nothing to do now but to go up and read. They had chosen the oil lamps carefully, ensuring they were heavy and solid-based, not liable to tip over or be knocked over easily. The fire risk was minimal, especially as the house was built from Cornish granite. It was the future which kept Louisa Jordan awake, not regret for the past, that and missing the rest of the family. If only she could have foreseen what would happen she could easily have prevented it. But it was too late and she would never forgive herself for the damage she had done to more than one person.

She slid home the bolts on the back door and went upstairs to bed.

Miranda Penhaligon lay in her single bed listening to the wind. It sighed through the rooftops between the obsolete chimney-pots and rocked the tangle of television aerials. Several streets away the Thames would be sludgy and rippled, no more than that, nothing so severe as the waves which would be crashing over the Cornish coastline leaving a litter of stones and seaweed, nylon rope and crates which had been swept overboard from fishing-boats. The wind might whip at hemlines and come at you in gusts at a corner but it didn't tear at your hair and bring stinging tears to your eyes. It was meeker in the city, as if it lived the half-life Miranda had become accustomed to. How I miss Cornwall, she thought, and how I miss them all, Joel especially.

London was all right for a while but the novelty had palled. Miranda had imagined that its population would make use of all the entertainment that was on offer but the girls she worked with went home most evenings to eat and watch television, only going out at the weekend with boyfriends or other girls.

She turned on her side. After fifteen months she still had trouble getting to sleep. There was no true darkness, no silence and stillness here. Traffic all through the night, rumbling taxis, their fares slamming the doors, lorries and cars and early morning road sweepers. And streetlights.

Tears filled her eyes. 'I can't bear it,' she whispered although there was no one to hear her. 'I want to go home.'

On Thursday morning, puffy-eyed, she dressed in her city clothes, ate some cereal and clattered down the stairs of the building in which her flat was situated. At the end of the street she jumped on a bus and squeezed in between two other people on a long side seat. Ten minutes later she got off and headed towards a tall building of whitish stone and lots of glass. The offices of an insurance company where her role was not clearly defined. Miranda had no qualifications and guessed she had got the job because she was decorative and good with people over the telephone.

At her desk she switched on the computer terminal and typed a letter of resignation. One month. She would give them the month they were due, they had, after all, been fair to her, then she would leave. Besides, she needed some time, she had to plan ahead.

'Morning.'

Miranda looked up. Standing in front of her was the only

cause for regret. Michael Hanson. It was his smile which had first attracted her, and then his personality. They had been seeing each other out of office hours for four months.

'A little wistful this morning?' He leant towards her, his hands on the edge of the desk. She could smell his aftershave.

'Just tired.'

He shook his head. 'It doesn't show. You always look good to me. Shall I get you a coffee?'

'Please.' She watched him retreat. Loose-limbed, confident and very sexy but her choice had been made.

Michael returned and placed the two plastic containers in their flimsy holders in front of her. He knew something was wrong and wondered if he was responsible. Miranda Penhaligon was not the first woman he had been serious about but she was the first one he didn't want to lose. She was almost as tall as himself, and as slender. Her skin was olive, her eyes dark brown, which was an odd but striking combination with her honey-coloured hair. She looked somehow foreign but when he had said so she had laughed and told him she was Cornish.

'Hence the name,' she had added, saying she was surprised he had not recognised her accent. But she had come to realise that, thanks to bad imitations by television actors and a lack of concern about the West Country in general, everyone who lived the other side of Bristol was considered to be some sort of Somerset-speaking rustic farmhand by those who lived in London.

'Look, let me take you out tonight, somewhere special.'

'Yes,' she said. 'I'd like that.'

Michael grinned and walked away. He had expected a refusal. That was another thing about Miranda, she was far from predictable.

Names and numbers came up on her screen. Miranda tried to concentrate, made herself do so, but all the time she was thinking about what she would tell Michael over dinner and how he would take it.

When the working day was over her head ached but she would not back out. Her mind was made up. She had placed her resignation letter in an envelope and left it on her manager's desk. During the afternoon he had called her in and asked why she wasn't happy with them.

'It isn't that. It's silly, I know, but I'm homesick.' He had not been able to understand it nor had he been able to persuade her to stay.

And now she must tell Michael because, in the way of all offices, the news would travel fast. He mustn't hear it from someone else.

The London bus lumbered through the streets so slowly she might just as well have walked. People got on and off, singly and in groups, some laughing with the relief of another day of work being over. Christmas lights shone in some of the shop windows but not overhead yet. She would still be there for the switching-on ceremony. Crowds thronged the pavements, homeward-going workers, shoppers with carrier bags, tourists and people wanting a meal before the theatre. And I won't miss any of it, she realised with a sense of freedom. All I want is to walk by the sea, to hear it crashing against the shore, to feel the wind in my hair and smell the salt in the air. And more than that, I want to see my mother.

But Michael first. She would shower and change and break it to him gently. I don't want to hurt him, she thought, knowing it to be true. If he loved her, which she suspected he did, she would not be able to avoid it. But if she stayed she might hurt him more. Either way she couldn't win.

CHAPTER THREE

At five to nine Rose said, 'Okay, you can pack up now. What I'd like you to do for me for next week is a still life. I know it might sound boring, and it certainly isn't my favourite art form, but it's still good discipline. Choose one household object and sketch it. Keep it simple, a plain background, and concentrate on the lines and perspective. We've all seen paintings of a bowl of apples or a jug on a table, but it isn't as easy as it looks. And don't forget the direction of light and shadows. That's it, then. See you all again next week.'

Chairs clattered and conversations began, noisy after the near silence of the last two hours. Friendships had been formed during the six weeks the course had been running. Rose knew who gave whom a lift and those who walked part of the way home together. Harry Osborne, a retired widower, waited alone at the front of the building inside the glass doors until his taxi arrived to carry him off. She was thinking of him, wondering if he was lonely, when Joel came over and made his strange request. She listened patiently, nodded, and found herself agreeing to do as he had asked.

When the last of her varied bunch of students had left, Rose turned down the heating and locked up.

In any group there was always one outsider, one person who did not and never would fit. Humoured or tolerated, ignored or ridiculed, there was no way to draw them into the natural cohesion which usually formed between those who shared a common interest. Joel Penhaligon was such a one, but Joel had talent and he had stamina and Rose had recognised that from the start. It was this which set him apart from the others. Of the eclectic group who turned up each week he was also the youngest. She was interested in him and his work but he was not an easy person to talk to. He was as Cornish as his name, with the squat muscular body, swarthy skin and near-black curly hair of his ancestors. Neither ugly nor handsome but pleasant-faced, Rose decided. When he smiled, which wasn't often, there was a hint of mischief about him. Hundreds of people came to Cornwall to paint, to capture the light and colours peculiar only to the Penwith peninsula, but Joel was a true Cornish artist.

She checked the door and stepped out into the street where the wind shrieked and snatched at her hair and almost knocked her sideways.

'You look as if you could do with a drink. But then I suppose that's nothing new.'

Rose spun around in surprise then smiled. 'If you're buying.' It was typical of her friendship with Barry Rowe that he would turn up without warning and offer to buy her a drink. It was a friendship which, like hers and Laura's, had spanned almost three decades beginning from the time before she married David and lasting after his long illness and death from cancer. 'Where to? The Navy?'

'Suits me. It's on the way for both of us.'

They walked down the hill away from the draughty room attached to the side of Geoff Carter's gallery which he loaned to Rose and various other artists on several nights a week. Rose had studied the work on show and liked it. It was full of life and feeling. Soon she would pay another visit to the Tate in St Ives where more modern art was on display. There was sculpture, too, including the work of Barbara Hepworth. Rose liked to keep abreast with local culture.

Barry Rowe was aware how full Rose's life had become and tried not to let his jealousy show, a feat he had never quite managed to achieve. He had never been in with a chance, not even before she met David, but he was always there, always at hand to pick up the pieces because that was where he liked to be. Just lately he felt she was drifting away from him. Success had done that; not altered her, Rose was Rose and that was that, but now her medium was oils her paintings were selling better than ever and there was this evening class, another new venture. She continued to produce work for him, although nowhere near as much as before.

The steeply sloping pavement was narrow, room enough only for one. Barry walked behind Rose who, short and slim, appeared smaller than ever in her padded jacket. Her wavy auburn hair, left loose that night, was lifted from her shoulders as the strong wind blew straight in their faces. On her feet were walking boots and thick red socks into which her jeans were tucked. From behind she might almost have been a child.

They were nearly at the bottom of Queen Street, the sea was directly ahead of them. They could hear it before they saw it as it rolled in, the high tide imminent, each wave slapping the Esplanade wall with a bomb-like crump followed by a splash as the tops of the waves and fingers of seaweed hit the paving stones and ran into the road.

A salvage tug swung on its anchor, its lights bright against the black sky. These tugs came and went, staying for days or for months, disappearing to refuel or to perform their function which was always to someone else's cost.

Spray hit them, carried by the wind across the width of the road. Barry pushed open the door of the pub and held it for Rose. It was warm inside and there were a dozen or more customers seated round the L-shaped bar talking or watching the football match being played silently on the television at the far end. Music came from a CD player, sixties music from the days of Rose and Barry's youth.

Gwyn, the landlady, greeted them by name. 'The usual?' she asked as she reached for a pint glass.

'Please.' Barry pulled a handful of change from his pocket, reaching beneath his threadbare donkey jacket to do so.

Rose shook her head. It was probably the same one he had worn when she first knew him.

They sat at the table in the corner by the window. Rose got out her cigarettes.

'I still don't know why you don't give up. You only smoke a couple a day.'

'And I enjoy every single one of them. Don't nag.' She blew smoke at the ceiling, which was adorned with naval artefacts. The light caught the glints in her hair which rested on her shoulders, tangled by the boisterous elements. And I've given up nagging you about smartening yourself up, she thought, although she had done so mercilessly in the past.

'How're the classes going?'

'Quite well now everyone's settled down. I'm beginning to spot which of them have any talent.' Joel Penhaligon, especially, she thought. It seemed an age since August when Geoff Carter had suggested she take the overflow from one or two of the other artists who passed on their skills in the annexe of his gallery.

'I'm not qualified, I don't know a thing about teaching,' Rose had told him, panicking at the suggestion. He had held an exhibition for her. Was this the payback? No, Geoff wouldn't have risked his own reputation if he didn't think she was good and besides, although he wasn't an artist himself, he liked to encourage those who were or might turn out to be.

'Of course you are. You were an art student yourself once. And you certainly know how to paint. It's not like council-run evening classes, you don't need qualifications. You've got four weeks to prepare yourself and I'm sure you won't want to disappoint any budding artists. Look, they'll be total novices wanting to learn the basics. They won't know charcoal from crayon. Just teach 'em one end of a pencil from the other and let them get on with it. And you'll be getting paid,' he'd added with a grin. So she had agreed and was glad to have done so even if it was only Joel who went any further.

'Why so glum?' Rose asked, aware that Barry was staring into his drink in his usual lugubrious stoop-shouldered manner.

'No reason.' But he was thinking she had more or less given up on the watercolours of flowers and local coves and villages which he reproduced on notelets and greetings cards and then sold from his shop. And photography. Only rarely now did she photograph scenes for the postcard side of the business. Oils had become her passion, one which had been submerged during the years of her marriage and until recently.

'Oh, did I tell you I've got a commission? I went to see the people yesterday.'

'No. Where? Local?'

'Sort of. Bodmin Moor, actually.'

Barry grinned. 'You call that local? And David always told me you were more Cornish than the Cornish. You know perfectly well that anywhere east of Hayle is considered foreign. Your Gloucestershire roots were showing there, maid. Anyway, what sort of commission?'

'A double portrait, I suppose you'd call it.'

Barry looked surprised. He took off his glasses with their thick tortoiseshell frames and polished them on the wide rib of his sweater in which there was a small hole. 'Do you think you're good enough?'

It was not an insult but a perfectly serious question. Barry knew as well as she did that being talented in one area of art did not mean you were competent all round. 'I think so.' It had been hard reverting to the smaller scale, more delicate work she was teaching her students after the strong, almost all-arm movements of her more dramatic work on canvas. During the first couple of lessons she had felt not only nervous but clumsy, but it was good discipline for her, as well as for them, especially working with pastels which smudged so easily. 'One portrait but two sitters. Sisters. The house is superb and they seem to have money. One's never married, the other one's husband did a bunk. Perhaps his money has provided for them.' Rose shrugged. 'Anyway, the older woman's about sixty but it's harder to guess the age of the other one.'

'What, older than you and me?'

'Thank you, dear. But I'm in my prime, you realise. And so are you.' But Barry had always seemed older than his years. His thinning hair and skinny body added to that impression.

'I don't think I've ever been in my prime,' he said so solemnly that Rose had to stop herself from laughing.

She finished her drink and stared, unseeing, down the length of the bar. 'There's something odd about the set-up. Why pick me and why have it done anyway?'

'Rose, don't. Lots of sisters live together and lots of people would like their portrait done if they could afford it. You just said they've got money.'

'I expect you're right.' She paused. 'And there's something else.'

Barry groaned. He had never known a woman so intent upon becoming involved in things which did not concern her. He wondered if another drink was called for before he heard what it was.

'My round,' Rose said, anticipating his thoughts. She slipped out from behind the table and went to the bar to get it.

'Something else, you said?' he asked when she sat down.

'Mm.' she sipped her wine. 'One of my students wants me to speak to his parents.'

'His?' He could not help the tiny stab of jealousy.

'He's very talented and wants a career in the arts only his father's against it on principle.'

'And this young man believes you can talk his father round?'

'That's about the strength of it.'

'And, naturally, you couldn't mind your own business and say no.'

Rose's eyes narrowed. A spiteful Barry did not make the best of company. 'No, I couldn't. I might be his only chance and he could go far. Surely you'd do the same in my position.'

'I expect I probably would.' Don't be churlish, he told himself. Rose will always get the better of you. 'When are you going to see this man?'

Rose shrugged. 'Joel's going to ring me.'

'You gave this boy your telephone number?' Barry's voice had risen in disbelief. 'You hardly even know him.'

'My number's in the book, dear, he could have found it for himself. Why are you being so unreasonable tonight?'

Because I'm a sad old bastard and I want you to myself, he admitted, but silently. 'I'm tired, or else it's the weather. Now, shall I walk you home?'

An odd comment for a man who never noticed the

weather, but Rose decided to let it go. 'No, I'll be fine, thanks.' She was hungry. She didn't eat before the class because it was too early and she did not like rushing a meal. If Barry walked her all the way back to Newlyn she would feel obligated to ask him in for a drink and if she didn't eat soon her appetite would diminish. There was haddock that night, already dipped in egg and breadcrumbs ready to grill. Vegetables, too, had been prepared. The Newlyn fishing fleet landed an annual catch greater than anywhere else in England and amounting to millions of pounds. Rose knew many of the fishermen, which meant there were times when she had more fish than she could eat. Laura had helped deplete her stock last night despite her protests about being satiated with seafood. But Laura could out-eat anyone. She thrived on nervous energy and remained thin to the point of skinniness.

Barry helped Rose on with her jacket and walked with her as far as the Queen's Hotel. The wind threatened to blow them over as it was funnelled round the corner where they said their goodbyes. Barry turned right, away from the seafront, into Morrab Road which would take him uphill, back into town the long way around. He lived in a small flat over his shop in a side street just off the centre of Penzance.

Rose turned to wave then carried on the way they had been walking, staying on the opposite side of the road from the Promenade in order not to get wet. The waves were higher now, sweeping across the protective wall of the carpark; there had been houses there once, but the sea had destroyed them in a vicious storm. Spray hissed as it flew skywards before splashing on the ground. Outside the

Mount's Bay Inn she hesitated only a second. Tempting as it was to sit by the fire and have one more drink before calling a taxi she decided to leave it for another night. Food was more important, and so was the exercise.

The dim glow from the hall light, set on a timing device, showed through the sitting room window. It enabled her to open the kitchen door, the entrance she always used, without fumbling in the dark for the right key. She went inside, flicked the switch for the strip-light and lit the gas under the pans containing vegetables. They would take longer to cook than the fish. Once she had laid the table – cork place mat, knife and fork, pepper and salt and tartare sauce – she poured a glass of wine and went through to the sitting room. The red light on the answering-machine blinked rapidly. There were three calls. The first from her mother who had been out when she rang to tell her the news the previous day. She looked at her watch. Ten thirty-five, too late to ring back now. Her parents were retired farmers but early nights and early rising was a habit ingrained and had never been broken.

She let the tape play on. 'Rose, it's Jack. Just a quick call to see how you are. I've been up to my eyes lately so I haven't had a chance to get in touch. Give me a ring when you can, tonight if possible. Cheers.'

Rose took another sip of her drink. She was standing in the dark, staring out over the bay. The sky was inky, the sea half a shade lighter. The tops of the waves were white with spume as they rushed frantically towards the shore. The lights on the salvage tug dipped and swayed. Other lights, those of Newlyn, shone to her left, those of

Marazion glittered ahead of her, distorted by distance. The Mount was a darker shadow against the sky

Jack Pearce. Detective Inspector Jack Pearce. One-time lover, now an occasional lover who wanted to be more. Tall, dark and handsome, classically good-looking, a man who could make her laugh, but also a man who could irritate her and who sometimes tried to control her. A thorn in her side. He would still be up but she didn't feel in the mood to speak to him.

The third voice was also instantly recognisable. Geoff Carter. With relief she heard him say he had sold another of her paintings. She had imagined something was wrong, that maybe she had not locked up properly. There were still times when she lacked confidence in herself and her abilities.

All three will have to wait, she decided, and went to put the fish under the grill.

As Rose ate, her thoughts went back Louisa and Wendy. There was a family resemblance between them, although not strong, but Wendy in particular reminded her of someone else. A week tomorrow she would see them again. When she made the preliminary sketches she might recognise who it was.

In the bedroom, warmed by central heating, she wondered why if they had the money, the Jordan sisters did not allow themselves much comfort. All that raking of fires and seeing to the range, Rose thought. It seemed more like a punishment than a way of life. Then she began to wonder if, perhaps, it was.

Rose got into the large wooden bed with its crisp white

cotton sheets and the gaily patterned patchwork quilt her mother had made. She had made no attempt to modernise the room, any alterations would have ruined its appeal. The walls were painted white, the carpet and curtains were a teddy-bear brown and the dressing-table was carved from the same shade of oak as the bed. A deep cupboard was set into the wall. It was where Rose hung her clothes. The only addition in over a hundred years had been the small radiator set against one wall.

She closed her eyes. A car passed, then another, otherwise there were no sounds except for the wind and the sea as it crashed against the rocks below the level of the road. A solitary black-backed gull called as it flew out to sea but by then Rose was asleep.

CHAPTER FOUR

'Good gracious. What do you make of this?' The *Western Morning News* was spread open on Wendy's lap. They had been shopping in Bodmin where they had also picked up the paper because no newsagent would deliver that far out. Beneath her tweed skirt Wendy's legs were encased in black ribbed tights. A red mohair sweater lent colour to her otherwise pale face. She jabbed a finger at the single paragraph, causing the paper to crackle.

Leaning over the side of the chair Louisa read the few short lines. 'How strange. Fancy someone trying to find him after all this time. I wonder why?' Seeing his name in print unsettled her and she needed a few minutes in which to think. The brass carriage clock on the half-moon table chimed the quarter hour. One fifteen. Lunch, later than usual, but the perfect excuse to escape.

In the kitchen Louisa buttered bread and made ham salad sandwiches as she thought of various reasons why solicitors might want Frank to contact them. The room was warm and cosy and a bacon joint which had been simmering on the range since breakfast added its meaty smell to that of the raw onions Wendy had chopped earlier for the sauce which would accompany it.

'Shall we have a drink with our lunch?'

Louisa looked up. Wendy stood in the kitchen doorway, leaning against the jamb as if she was weak. 'Good idea. It might buck us up a bit. Shopping always tires me.' She smiled, aware that Wendy, who had always been the more serious one, worried about life far more than she did herself. 'I really fancy a gin and vermouth. Can we run to that?'

'Gin and It? That takes me back. But I don't think we've got any olives.' She went to pour the drinks and carried them back to the kitchen. There was no ice because, without electricity, there was no way in which to freeze cubes. The larder, a one-storey extension, had a flagstone floor and marble shelves and ensured food did not perish as long as they shopped on a regular basis. Both sisters admitted this gave them something to do.

Louisa pushed a plate towards Wendy then took a sip of her drink. 'Mm, delicious. Remember how Frank and I always had one before dinner?' Seeing his name in the paper had brought back the memory.

'I do.' Wendy had been a frequent visitor to the house in Penzance. Frank might have poured the drinks but it was his day he talked about, never his wife's. I always knew him for what he was, she thought, but Louisa seemed to love him so I kept quiet. But she had been there, near at hand, for the times when things went wrong, which they had done frequently. 'Louisa, did Frank have any relatives?'

'Relatives? As far as I can recall there were two ancient

aunts but he didn't keep in touch with them. Why?' She bit into the sandwich and hoped it wouldn't choke her. Why now? she kept asking herself.

'Because that's probably the answer. One or both have died and they've left him some money. How hard do you think they'll look for him?'

'I don't know. And, Wendy, I don't really care. Whatever the reason, it can't affect us now.' The house they had owned in Penzance had been in Louisa's name; its sale and the purchase of her present home had been completed on the day of Frank's disappearance so there had been no problems about ownership. Both women had money of their own, Wendy's now supplemented by her old age pension and Louisa's by investments she had made over the years and a medium-sized win on the Premium Bonds. 'Do stop worrying, it's nothing to do with us. Now, if you're not going to eat that I'll put it out for the birds.' She finished her drink and said that as it was her turn to prepare the vegetables for dinner she might as well do so now.

'In that case I'll cut out that skirt I've been meaning to make for months.'

Louisa nodded. They both needed something to do, something to distract them from thoughts of Frank, and if they remained in the same room they would not be able to avoid talking about him. She turned to the sink and began peeling potatoes.

Rose woke at six-thirty and lay in bed listening. The wind had dropped but rain lashed against the casement window in bursts. 'Bloody typical,' she said as she swung her legs over the side of the bed and stood up in one fluid movement. 'The one day I decide to give myself a treat and not work it pours with rain.' She shrugged because, on the other hand, no outdoor work would be possible anyway in such a downpour.

The telephone was ringing. She went downstairs to answer it before the machine cut in.

'Rose? It's me.'

'Laura?' The voice most familiar to her was hardly more than a vaguely recognisable croak.

'I can't make it today I feel like death.'

'It doesn't matter, especially in this weather. It wouldn't have been much fun. You sound dreadful. Go back to bed and stay there. Shall I come over?'

'No. I'll be okay and I can barely speak.'

'I'll call in later anyway and see how are you.' Flu, Rose thought as she filled the coffee machine with water. At least Laura could rest because Trevor was at sea.

The day had not started well; first the weather and now Laura. Rose decided to use the change of plan to advantage and type out some invoices and develop the roll of film still waiting upstairs. Occasionally she did some photography for old clients who insisted it was her services they wanted. The jobs were mainly commercial; building sites, factories or staff groups. Gone were the days when she took pictures of a baby's first birthday or a fiftieth wedding anniversary. She had to admit that she still enjoyed taking the shots for postcards when a wide-angle lens could capture a panoramic view of a harbour, a coastline or a cluster of cottages grouped around one of the numerous coves. But that was summer work.

Looking out of the kitchen window at the saturated lawn

she said, ''Es, my 'ansome, tiz real West Penwith weather,' in perfect imitation of Doreen Clarke, a more recent friend who lived in Hayle. She was due a visit any time now. It had been several weeks since she had called in for a chat.

Rose took her coffee into the sitting room and debated whether or not to light the fire. It would cheer the room up a bit, but if she was upstairs working, it would be pointless. 'What now?' The telephone rang for a second time. It was only just after seven but everyone knew she was an early riser.

'Hello?'

'Ah, there you are.'

'Where else did you expect me to be, Jack?'

'Don't snap. Oh, don't tell me, you've got a hangover.' She let out a deep sigh of exasperation.

'I have not. It was my class last night. What do you want?'

'It's nice to feel so loved,' he responded wryly. 'Did I wake you?'

'No.'

'Good. Look, I tried to get hold of you several times, I've got the day off. Fancy doing something? Not even you can work in this weather.' He waited. 'Rose? If you don't want to see me, just say so.'

She wasn't sure. She had already had one change of plan and felt vaguely irritable. Eight minutes past seven and Detective Inspector Jack Pearce had already managed to have that effect upon her. 'What did you have in mind?' she asked coolly.

'Lunch, shopping, a film, you name it.'

'Lunch then. I've got things to do this morning.' And he knows I hate shopping, she thought. 'I'll pick you up at twelve.'

'Okay.' Rose replaced the receiver. 'Oh, Jack. What is it about you?' She was always puzzled by the ambiguity of her feelings towards him.

The wind had changed direction. It now blew from the south and the rain pattered against the kitchen window; a more gentle rain, a warmer wind. Rose ate some toast then went upstairs to shower.

Half an hour later she mounted the flight of stairs which led from the creaking boards of the first-floor landing to the attic. She sat down, another mug of coffee to hand, and began typing with two fingers. One invoice was for Barry Rowe. She was shocked when she realised the photographs of the fishing village of Porthleven and those of Marazion had been taken over three months ago. Barry insisted they kept their business dealings on a business-like footing, she was getting sloppy.

By ten to twelve there were four envelopes sealed and stamped, ready to post, in her handbag. The roll of film, weighted at the bottom, was hanging by a clip in the drying cabinet and a crisp pile of ironing sat on the wooden slats of the airing-cupboard shelves. The smell of warm clothing lingered in the kitchen and Rose felt virtuous, deserving of lunch out.

'Very nice,' Jack said when he arrived, tapping on the window before letting himself in.

Nice. Typical Jack. Rose thought she looked rather fetching in a long-sleeved wool dress, heeled shoes and make-up. 'Where're you taking me?'

'How about Truro? I know you like the wine bar.'

'Meaning?' She picked up her bag and keys.

'Dear God, woman, meaning nothing. Why're you always so teasy?'

'You make me that way,' she said over her shoulder as she hurried down the drive to the car. Jack had parked in the road which led from Mousehole to Newlyn. Other cars queued behind it as they waited for the oncoming traffic to pass. 'Typical policeman, you think you can park anywhere you like,' Rose said as she got into the passenger seat.

Jack shook his head. He was beginning to wish she'd refused his invitation.

Once they were on the dual carriageway Rose told him about Louisa and Wendy.

She's relenting, he thought, she just cannot resist my charm.

He did not know how right he was. From time to time Rose glanced at his profile. She sometimes forgot how handsome he was, how his nearness affected her. 'I've no idea how those women heard of me, although they did say they'd bought one of my paintings.'

'Why don't you ask them? You're not usually averse to interrogating people.'

She turned her head. Jack's eyes were on the road, but the faint smile was visible, even in profile. Perhaps he enjoyed the sparring as much as she did.

Truro was busy with shoppers but even their number could not dominate the city in the way in which the cathedral did. Built smack in the centre it towered over the shops which huddled within its precincts. They ducked between umbrellas as they made their way to the wine bar. It was only the second week in November but already shop windows were decorated for Christmas. Rose believed

December was early enough for such things.

They chose a table close to the bar and ordered their food and a bottle of Australian white wine. There was pasta for Jack and a Greek salad for Rose. Over lunch Jack talked mostly of the job and the big case they had been working on. Rose listened and refilled her glass twice as she wasn't driving. Not once did he mention their relationship. Perhaps he's accepted the way things are, she thought as he ordered coffee. Perhaps we can be good friends.

The wipers flicked backwards and forwards rhythmically as they drove back. It was warm in the car and Rose felt sleepy. She pressed the button to let down the window an inch or so. To her left a kestrel was hovering over the sloping ground below an old engine-house. It was near enough that she could see its pointed wings and long, barred tail. She pointed it out to Jack who could only take a quick look. 'How do you know it's not a sparrowhawk?' he asked.

'Sparrowhawks don't hover, they glide,' she answered dismissively as she reached for the national newspaper tucked under the dashboard.

By the time they pulled into Rose's drive it had stopped raining. Jack cut the engine and glanced across at Rose.

He had bought their lunch, it would seem rude not to invite him in. 'Coffee?' she said, turning to face him. His grin of pleasure made her feel good.

'Thanks.'

They went inside. Out over the bay the clouds were gathering again. The weather was as unsettled as Rose's mood. When I don't see him, I miss him, if he rings too often it annoys me. I must be terribly selfish, she realised as she made the coffee. Maybe I'm doing it all wrong, maybe I shouldn't have listened to Laura. Laura was a great believer in keeping a man on his toes. 'Once they see you're hooked they'll either get bored and leave you or else they'll start taking you for granted,' she had told Rose one night when they were exchanging confessions in the Swordfish bar. Well Rose certainly kept Jack on his toes.

'Is that why you and Trevor are always threatening to split up?' Rose had asked with a grin. It hadn't been like that with David. They had always shown each other consideration. But Jack wasn't David and that was the problem. Maybe some mental defence mechanism was at work, maybe she refused to get too close, to commit herself, because she could not bear the idea of losing someone she loved again.

There was a closed expression on Rose's face. Jack wondered what had caused it. 'When are you going back to Bodmin?' he asked, hoping to gain her interest.

Rose joined him at the kitchen table. 'Next Thursday. We've agreed on one session a week.'

'I hope it goes well for you.'

She saw that he meant it. 'Thank you.'

To her surprise Jack didn't stay long. She had imagined he would prolong the visit to encompass supper. But he stood up, stretched, then bent to kiss her on the cheek. He smelt of soap and lunchtime garlic. 'I have to go. I'm meeting up with some old mates from CID in Plymouth. They're only down here for one night.'

Rose raised one eyebrow and grinned. 'I hope you're stocked up with paracetamol.' She could envisage the evening ahead. 'And don't stay out too late, you know you can't stand the pace any more.' One up to me, she thought, because every time Jack caught her with a glass of wine in her hand he made her feel guilty by his judgemental silence or accused her of almost becoming an alcoholic. It was so unfair, he just always happened to pick the moment she decided to pour a drink to turn up.

She watched him go out to the car. It was dark now and the air was damp but his firm features and thick hair were lit briefly by the interior light as he opened the door. He waved then reversed down the drive, tooting once when he reached the bottom to warn any traffic approaching from his left.

Rose had neglected Laura. She rang her, hoping she wasn't asleep. 'How do you feel?'

'Better than I did this morning.'

'You sound it. Do you need any shopping? Can I cook you a meal?'

'To be honest, I'm better on my own. I'm sitting by the fire reading and I've been drinking plenty of fluids.'

'Well, if you're sure. I'll be over tomorrow for certain.' Rose returned to the kitchen, pulled down the blind and looked at her watch. She smiled, she was also glad to be on her own. 'And talking of fluids – yes. Why not? It's after six and the sun's definitely over the yardarm.' She rummaged in the untidy drawer next to the sink and retrieved the corkscrew. 'Here's to the portrait,' she said as she took the first sip of wine.

In front of her own fire, which she had decided to light, Rose listened to the crackling logs as she turned the pages of the *Western Morning News,* skimming through articles rather than reading them properly. Only when the name Jordan appeared in a small paragraph did a frown of concentration bisect her brow. It was a coincidence, of course, even if Jordan was not a terribly common name. But Louisa's husband had left her and they had avoided talking about him, making it plain that personal topics were taboo.

Shadows danced across the room, lit only by the table lamp by Rose's side. She got up and went to the window. The sitting room curtains were never drawn, she could not bear to shut out that view no matter what time of day it was. Over the bay stars glittered in the gaps between clouds. To her left and below her, Rose could see men on the quay. A boat must have returned, not Trevor's, but someone else's husband and crew safely home again. They would land the fish in the morning. One or more would sleep on the trawler until it was time to do so. How different their lives were from those of Louisa and Wendy. With sadness she recalled the lines written on the walls of South Crofty, the last mine to close. 'Cornish lads are fishermen, and Cornish lads are miners, too, but when the fish and tin have gone what are the Cornish boys to do?' But the tin has gone, she thought, and there isn't much else left. Except for people such as the Jordans and Penhaligons. Why should that be?

'You always make mysteries out of nothing,' Barry Rowe once told her. She suspected she was doing so again. But her thoughts were interrupted by the telephone. It was Joel Penhaligon ringing to ask if she could possibly spare the time to speak to his father tomorrow evening.

'I'll come with you,' Michael Hanson said quite seriously the day after Miranda had broken the news. He had insisted on taking her out again in order to try to change her mind.

Miranda stared at him, her pretty face expressing shock. 'You can't just give up your job. Besides, there's no work down there. Any you found would pay abysmally after what you've been earning here.' But she was flattered and tempted by the offer.

'But you're going back.'

'It's different for me.'

'How?' He leant across the table of the Covent Garden bistro where they had eaten. 'I've got family there.'

'And I'll have you. You can't stay with them for ever. Look, Miranda, if you don't want to see me any more, tell me.'

'I do,' she whispered. 'I do. But I want to go home too.' She ran a hand through the tangle of fair curls. Each of her fingers was encircled by a delicate silver ring. 'It's not like here, you have to understand that. It's not like anywhere else at all. The people are different, the whole way of life is different. You've only known me a couple of months, you can't throw everything up on the strength of that.' Could someone like Michael appreciate the winters, could he ever come to love the hot summers the way she did? She would have given anything to be walking along the beach at that moment, to hear the sea rushing shorewards, hissing as it flowed over the pebbles before receding with a sucking noise. How those sounds soothed her.

'Miranda, are you in some sort of trouble?'

She looked away. The question was too near the mark.

'Are you?'

She raised her head. There was concern in his kind face and the small scar at the corner of his mouth added interest to his good looks. She suspected that she loved him. 'In trouble. What makes you ask that?'

'I don't know.' He pushed at some crumbs on the tablecloth. 'I've always had the feeling you came to London to escape something, and now you feel it's safe to go back. Am I right? Was it a man?'

'Sort of,' she said, for it was true, but not in the way Michael had meant.

A waiter approached their table. The long, white apron wrapped around his middle almost concealed the black trousers he wore beneath it. He cleared their plates, making no comment about the amount of food left on them. He was experienced, he had seen it all before. A lover's argument soon depleted appetites and these two did not look at all happy.

'We'll just have the bill, please,' Michael said, trying to smile.

The restaurant felt stuffy to Miranda, and the mixed cooking smells, overridden by herbs, made her feel nauseous. All around them was cheerful conversation, the chink of cutlery on crockery and intermittent bursts of laughter. She suddenly felt lonely. I'll soon be twenty, she thought, and I already feel old. Youth and innocence had been taken from her and could never be replaced. 'Excuse me.' She stood as Michael pulled out the table to allow her room to manoeuvre.

In the Ladies she leant her forehead against the cold, gleaming white tiles. A sick headache had taken hold. That's all I need, she thought. But the nausea subsided when she splashed her face with water. In the mirrored

58

wall behind the wash-basins her reflection stared back at her. It might have been that of a stranger for she no longer knew herself. She had paid to have her thick hair fall in wild curls and she had bought new clothes, office clothes; smart skirts and jackets and feminine blouses. She had also learnt to apply subtle make-up. But underneath it all was the same Miranda, the same teenage girl who had worn jeans with threadbare knees, her hands deep in the pockets of a red reefer jacket as she had walked on the sand in winter thinking of her future. How different that future had become. No university, no fun, only a constant feeling of doom and a longing for home. Could she burden Michael with the half-person she had become? It would hardly be fair. But neither could she tell him what had made her that way.

She washed her hands and made use of the almond-scented hand lotion standing on the vanity unit then returned to the table where Michael was waiting with her coat.

'Come home with me,' she said in the taxi. 'Come home and make love to me.'

Michael stroked her hair. He probably wouldn't. Miranda needed comfort, not sex. He wished he knew why.

CHAPTER FIVE

Rose shook her head. Why was it that the telephone only rang when she was in the bath, about to leave the house or had already left it? But the same law seemed to apply to everyone. With her bags and keys in her hand she retraced her steps across the kitchen and into the sitting room to answer it.

'Some weather, eh? We don't know where we are, it's neither this, that nor the third thing.' Doreen Clarke did not give her a chance to give her name or number, she simply assumed she was talking to Rose. 'It don't do much for Cyril, not when he can't get out in the garden.'

Rose waited. There was no point in interrupting, Doreen would get to the point in her own time. A peculiar sort of friendship had developed between the two women although all they had in common was their age. Cyril was an ex-miner; he had been made redundant when Wheal Jane was closed and had not worked since. He and Doreen owned their small stone bungalow in Hayle and she took on cleaning jobs to make ends meet. Doreen looked ten years older than her age. A short, dumpy woman with straight grey hair cut just below ear level, she dressed frumpily and with a disregard for fashion. She was honest and down-to-earth and a wonderful source of gossip as there were few people she did not know or know of within the area.

'Cyril's real fond of you, maid, he'd never say so, of course, not my Cyril. Well, he never says much anyway. But it's not everyone he's so generous with his vegetables.'

Rose tried not to laugh. It sounded like an old music hall joke. And Cyril didn't say much because he rarely got a chance to.

'He's got some lovely cabbages and carrots. If you're in tomorrow morning I'll drop 'un over.'

'Thank you. About ten?'

'Suits me fine. I likes to get me bits done early. Cheers now.'

Rose hung up. That takes care of at least an hour, she thought, knowing Doreen would have completed her shopping by then and would linger over coffee. The weekly Saturday visit to Penzance had been a ritual since the days of her childhood when she rode over on the bus with her mother.

Rose's destination was Zennor but first she would call in and see Laura. Laura answered the door in her dressing gown. Her face was white, her eyes dull and the mass of dark corkscrew curls was lank. 'Coffee?' she croaked.

'Yes, but I'll make it.' After nearly thirty years Rose was almost as comfortable in her friend's house as she was in her own. It seemed astonishing that Laura and Trevor had brought up three boisterous boys in the cramped accommodation but in previous eras fishermen had had larger families than that and managed. 'For you,' Rose said, indicating the plastic bag she had placed on the worktop.

Laura opened it. There were satsumas, a lemon and bananas, throat sweets and a half-bottle of whisky. She hugged Rose. 'Thank you.'

'The whisky's for later, with the lemon and hot water. I won't stay long, you look as if you should be in bed. Have you seen the doctor?'

'No, but I rang that number where they put you on to a nurse. They said there was no point because he wouldn't prescribe anything for flu, just to keep warm, drink plenty and ride it out.'

'Then do it. When's Trevor back?'

'He's landing on Monday. I should be over it by then.'

Rose finished her coffee and left, promising to call in again. 'Leave a message if there's anything you want.'

She saw herself out and set off for Zennor, a picturesque village with one pub, a museum and its church famous for the mermaid carving. It was also the place where D. H. Lawrence had once lived with his German wife, Frieda, until the locals, aided by the constabulary, had driven them out, accusing them of signalling German U-boats by way of washing hanging on the line. Not that any U-boats had ever been known to lie off the shore.

Doreen was right, the weather was so variable it was hard to decide what to wear each day. Rose, however, was in her working uniform of jeans, thick shirt, jumper, bodywarmer and wool socks and boots. Over this would go the waxed jacket she kept on the back seat of the car and which had served her well and still remained waterproof even if it was scruffy.

The sky was clear and blue but the wind came from the east. There had been a hint of frost in the night. Bodmin Moor would have been white with it, the stiffened bracken like stalagmites. Rose wondered how Wendy and Louisa would cope if they were snowed in. It had happened before. Helicopters had had to drop supplies to farmers and those living in isolation whilst down on the coast the temperature would remain several degrees above freezing, which did not stop West Penwithians from complaining of the cold.

Rose parked and walked back up the steep hill carrying her gear. She was warm from the effort by the time she found a sheltered spot at the top where she sat at right angles to the sea. For ten minutes she contemplated her surroundings. The sea was chlorophyll green, capped with white. A dot on the horizon might have been a cargo boat. Inland lay the slopes of the hills with their winter browns and greens, a couple of granite buildings just visible. Smoke rose from one of the chimneys and was sent zigzagging by the wind. Below was the village, the roofs of houses in steps, and, of course, the church. There were no songbirds now, only the call of a gull or the croak of a crow broke the silence.

That's how I'll paint it. Rose decided, half land, half sea. In her fingerless gloves she began to work and continued to do so until the approaching dusk drained the blueness from the sky. She collected up apple cores, flask, ground sheet and equipment and walked back to the car, slightly stiff from sitting for so long.

Only when she stepped into the warmth of the house did she realise how cold she had been. As she rinsed the flask and stacked her gear in the larder which led off the kitchen, her extremities began to tingle. There was just time to eat a banana, drink a cup of tea and change before setting off to pick up Joel. She had offered to meet him at his school but he had said he would walk up to Penwith College and wait for her there to save her a diversion. The bulk of school and college traffic would have dispersed by now. It would take no more than a few minutes to reach him. Wearing a skirt and jumper and the good tan woollen coat and boots, Rose set off.

Joel was standing on the pavement, a bag over his shoulder, his hands in his pockets. He appeared younger and more vulnerable than he did during her classes. She reminded herself he was only seventeen.

'Hi,' he said when Rose pulled in and he'd got into the passenger seat.

He seems nervous, she thought, is his father that much of a tyrant?

'Thanks, again, Mrs Trevelyan. If Miranda had been around I wouldn't have had to ask you to do this.'

'Miranda?'

'My cousin. She disappeared about a year ago. She was more like a sister than a cousin.'

Disappeared? What now? Rose asked herself. 'How old is she?'

'Nineteen now, eighteen at the time.'

A sixth sense told her she would somehow become

64

involved with this family, more so than she was already. Sixth sense, or experience. 'What happened?'

'No one knows. At the end of August last year she was still living at home with her parents, my aunt and uncle. My father's sister and her husband. They'd put the house up for sale but the morning they were due to move Uncle Frank disappeared, he just walked out without warning, and the next thing I heard was Miranda had gone, too. She was supposed to be going to university at the end of the holidays. I've never heard from her since. I was really hurt, I still am, I thought we were so close. Anyway, she's not here to stick up for me, so I asked you.' He grinned. 'I know it's ridiculous at my age, but there we are.'

'Why won't your father listen to you?'

'Oh, he listens, but he expects other things of me.'

Rose sighed. If the man was so entrenched in his opinions she would be wasting her time. Joel knew about student grants and work to be had during the vacations, she found it difficult to understand the real problem. He had the talent and she had thought he had the determination to follow his chosen career.

'I just want him to understand, that's all,' Joel said, as if he had read her thoughts. 'I want him to see that he can't dictate the course of my life and I'd like him on my side for once.'

'I'll do what I can. Your cousin, Miranda, you don't have any idea where she might've gone?'

'None. I'd seen her a couple of days previously. My aunt said she believed she'd gone with her father, but I knew that couldn't be true. They didn't get on that well. Louisa went anyway, alone, instead of it being the three of them. My father contacted the police because he didn't believe the tale about Miranda being with Uncle Frank, especially as she adored her mother.'

Louisa? Could this be Louisa Jordan? Yes. The piece in the paper said solicitors wanted to contact a Frank Jordan. It all fell into place. 'Is Frank's surname Jordan?'

'Yes. Do you know him?'

'No.' Rose concentrated on the road. Joel and his family may not be aware that solicitors were trying to trace him. 'What were you saying about the police?'

'Dad was worried something might have happened to Miranda. He'd gone over to help with the move and discovered Aunt Louisa on her own. He thought it all very odd.'

Louisa Jordan had made no mention of a daughter. In fact, she had stated that there was only herself and Wendy. Not only had she omitted to mention Miranda, it seemed as if she had forgotten the existence of her brother and his family as well.

'Well, like I said, this happened over a year ago and as we haven't heard anything it's possible she's now living with my aunts.'

'Wendy moved at the same time?'

'About a month or so later. She told Dad that whatever happened she knew Louisa would never take Frank back. She gave an estate agent the keys to her cottage and left him to sell it. Hang on, how do you know my other aunt's name?'

'I've met her. I've met them both. Let's leave it at that for the moment.'

Joel nodded. A few minutes later he said, 'Slow down, it's that gate up ahead.'

Rose indicated and turned into the driveway. The house was set back from the road and there was plenty of space to park. Even in the darkness of a winter's evening she saw that Joel's father had done well for himself. The large property was solid and impressive and electricity bills were no problem judging from the number of lights blazing in all the windows.

Joel let them in with his key. They could hear voices in the lounge behind a door to the right of the wide passageway. Rose had almost forgotten the purpose of her visit with all she had learnt in the car. If Miranda did live with her mother and her aunt, there were no signs of her presence in the house. But then, she might have gone to university after all.

Roger Penhaligon stood when they entered the high-ceilinged room. He was a big man. Ash fell to the carpet as he transferred his cigar to his left hand before offering his right one to Rose. 'Ah, Joel's friend. Pleased to meet you. I'm Roger, this is my wife, Petra.'

'Rose Trevelyan.' She smiled in Petra's direction. It seemed Joel had not told his parents who their visitor was. Petra looked worried whereas her husband appeared merely curious. Presumably they had been expecting a girlfriend.

'Mrs Trevelyan? Then you're Joel's art teacher. I'm sorry, we didn't realise. Please sit down.'

At least he now knew that much about her. Rose turned and sank into the deep, soft cushions of one of a matching pair of settees.

'Can we offer you a drink? I know you've got the car but one won't hurt.'

'Thank you. That would be nice. Dry white wine if you have it.'

'Petra? Would you mind?'

She was already halfway to her feet as if glad to have something to do.

'Joel said he was bringing someone home but he kept your identity a secret. Sit down, for goodness' sake,' he added, addressing his son who was hovering near the door.

The whole family seems to have secrets, she thought. 'Mr Penhaligon, I—'

'Oh, Roger, please.' Despite the admonishment of his son, Roger remained standing himself, one hand resting on the ornate mantelpiece, a relic of former times when workmanship was of a far higher quality. Beneath it logs burnt in the grate, adding to the comfortable ambience of the pleasantly decorated room. Roger's voice was deep, coarsened by whisky and cigars, but Rose did not find him intimidating.

'I'm here on Joel's behalf, at his request,' she began as Petra returned with a tray. There were four glasses, so they clearly had no objection to their son joining them in a drink. The interruption was well timed. Rose knew she had sounded a little pompous.

'On Joel's behalf?' Petra inquired as she poured wine and handed Rose a glass.

'He's very talented, Mrs Penhaligon. Extremely talented, in fact. It would be a terrible waste if he didn't go to art college.'

'I see.' Roger drew at the stub of his cigar, blew the smoke at the ceiling and threw the butt in the fire. 'What, precisely, has he told you about me?'

'Very little, I assure you, only that you object to his choice of career.'

'Ah, I see. The Victorian parent putting his foot down.'

Rose grinned. Roger Penhaligon had a sense of humour and could laugh at himself.

'Come, Joel, it's time you spoke up for yourself. Tell Rose what I've always told you.'

'That you want me to go to university then into one of the professions.'

Roger nodded as he stared, unseeing, at the crackling fire. 'Not in so many words, Joel. And what have you always said?'

'That I want to paint.'

'Quite. So what's to stop you? Afraid if you go to art college I won't keep you in luxury?'

Joel's face reddened. Petra looked from father to son but remained silent. Rose watched them all. She decided she rather liked Roger Penhaligon, that he had qualities his family might not appreciate, and she thought she understood what had been going on.

'You said I'd never make any money and you didn't want me hanging around with a crowd of hippies.'

Roger laughed. 'Hippies? Did I say that? I probably meant beatniks.'

Rose lowered her head to hide her grin. It was doubtful Joel had even heard of the word.

'Look, son. I think we're wasting Rose's time, although,'

he added, turning to her, 'it's been a pleasure to meet you. I know I've said there's plenty of time to come to a decision, but I accept that time is running out. You might not see it our way but we do have your interests at heart.

'I won't go on but if you're certain you want to paint then we won't stand in your way. We had to be sure you were sure. We wanted to put up all the objections, you see. But you haven't changed your mind and we can both see how determined you are. Now Rose has confirmed you have the necessary talent, in which case, I agree, it should not go to waste.'

Joel stared at his father then, stiffly, awkwardly, he got up and embraced him. 'Thanks,' he whispered.

'Did you not realise his potential?' Rose asked, knowing both males were embarrassed.

'I was never given a chance to. Joel has never shown us his work.'

The dynamics of family life fascinated her. How different the Penhaligons were from her own family. She had shown her parents everything she had committed to paper or canvas.

'Will you have another drink?' Roger asked.

'I'd better not, thanks.' Rose stood and reached for her handbag on the cushion beside her.

'Dad, Mrs Trevelyan seems to have heard of Uncle Frank.' Joel spoke quickly because he didn't want Rose to leave, he was terrified that all that his father had said had been for her benefit and as soon as the door closed behind her he would change his mind again.

'Really?' Roger's expression was puzzled.

'It's odd, but I met your sisters recently.'

'Good God. How on earth did you come across them? Look, are you sure you won't have another drink?'

'Half a glass,' she answered sensibly. Once it was in her hand she continued. 'They commissioned me to paint their portrait.'

'Whatever for?'

'I'm not really sure, they weren't very forthcoming.'

'No. They wouldn't be. When was this?'

'Recently. I haven't started it yet.'

'Then you know where they live.' It was Petra who spoke. Her voice was low with the slightest trace of a Cornish accent but it carried clearly. She might appear delicate but Rose guessed she, too, had inner strength.

'Yes.' This was embarrassing. If her clients did not want their brother to know how to find them she could not tell him.

Petra smiled. 'I can see your dilemma, Mrs Trevelyan, so we won't ask. We knew they were moving somewhere on Bodmin Moor but no more than that. Louisa and Wendy have our address and telephone number, it is up to them to make contact if they wish to.' She paused. 'May I ask you this? Is Miranda with them?'

'I honestly can't tell you. Neither of your sisters-in-law mentioned her and although I've only been in one room of the house there was no indication that a younger woman might live there.

'I believe you contacted the police,' she said to Roger.

'I did. It was all most peculiar. One minute a family of three is about to move house, the next there's only Louisa.

With Wendy following so quickly I wondered if it was all prearranged.' He shook his head. 'Miranda was of age, there was nothing anyone could do. I tried the universities to which she had applied but they couldn't help me either.'

'You were that worried?'

'Yes. We all loved Miranda. She spent a lot of her time with us and she was particularly devoted to Joel. I couldn't understand her not even writing to him. Still,' he shrugged, 'she's probably safe. No one's come back to us, there haven't been any reports of unidentified young women's bodies.

'How did you link my sisters to Joel?'

There was no point in hiding it. The article had been in the paper for anyone to see. Rose explained what she had read.

'Their marriage was unusual,' Petra said. 'I always felt Louisa could've been happier with someone else, yet she was devoted to Frank. I've always suspected he'd already found someone else and used the occasion as an excuse to get out.' She placed her glass on the small table beside her. 'But that still doesn't explain Miranda's disappearance.

'Mrs Trevelyan, I apologise for the impertinence, but if, by any chance, the conversation turns to children or families when you're with them, do you think you could discreetly find out anything you can?'

'I'll do my best.' A fairly ambiguous answer but Rose knew she would not be able to resist doing so. It was a challenge, and Louisa and Wendy couldn't possibly guess she knew the rest of their family. It really was time to leave. As she stood for the second time Rose saw in her mind the faces of both Jack and Barry and knew what they would think of her for becoming involved.

Hands were shaken again, Petra's grip was as firm as her husband's, then Petra showed Rose to the door. Joel remained silent but she saw by his face how grateful he was for her visit. At least some good came of it, she thought as she started the engine and pulled out into the road, wishing there was someone in whom she could confide. Not Laura, she was far from well, and certainly not Barry Rowe. Would Jack listen dispassionately or would he be in one of his stern, leave-it-alone moods? There was only one way to find out.

She glanced at the dashboard clock. It was early, not yet seven thirty. Pulling into a lay-by she dialled his home number on the mobile phone he'd insisted she took out with her at night and was pleased when he said he would meet her in the Mount's Bay Inn in twenty minutes. 'There's something I want to tell you,' he ended enigmatically.

He sounds really cheerful for once, Rose decided as she headed towards the seafront.

CHAPTER SIX

'You're pale, maid,' Doreen Clarke said as she bustled into the kitchen through the side door, a cardboard box in her arms. She had parked at the bottom of the drive and was breathless from the exertion of hurrying up the steep incline.

'There's a lot of flu about. I hope I haven't picked it up from Laura.' Rose was not physically ill, her pallor was due to lack of sleep, but she didn't want Doreen to know that.

Outside, reflecting her mood, the sky was grey once more. There was no wind, no force behind the weather, just a dismal bank of cloud cover. The garden, which Rose tended sporadically, needed some tidying. Droplets of earlier rain clung to the spiders' webs strung between straggling plants.

The garden looks no different from usual, Rose thought as she listened to Doreen's chatter. There've always been lumps in the lawn, I don't cut the grass often enough and I mostly forget to deadhead things. It just seems worse today somehow. The garden at the side of the house also overlooked the bay. Near the converted shed was a bench on which Rose spent many hours in the summer, as had Jack when they shared a

74

bottle of wine. Oh, bugger the man, she thought.

'No work today, dear?' Doreen asked as she removed her shapeless coat with its odour of damp wool and the patterned headscarf she was rarely without.

'No. Well, maybe later if the weather clears up. I'm now working for two ladies on Bodmin Moor, I'm doing their portraits.'

'Whatever for? 'Tis real vain, that sort of thing, if you ask me.' Doreen tucked her no-nonsense hair behind her ears and made herself comfortable at the table. Her snap-clasped handbag hung over the back of the chair. It was the sort the Queen tended to favour and probably the reason Doreen did too.

Rose smiled wanly. Typical Doreen, no congratulations, no interest in the clients, merely condemnation of something she did not understand. 'They used to live in Penzance.' If anyone knew of them it would be her friend, but Rose didn't want to break any confidences. Not that anyone had asked her to keep quiet and, in fact, Petra Penhaligon had encouraged her to ask questions.

'And what name do they go by?' Doreen spooned sugar into her coffee.

'Jordan. One of them, anyway.'

'Ah, well, they always had more money than sense. A friend of mine used to clean for Louisa. That was some years ago now, mind. She said you wouldn't believe the money they wasted on things that were not much use to anyone, object dart or some such thing they called them. A bit like this here portrait, I suppose.'

Rose wondered at the strange French pronunciation

but then, some of Doreen's English was equally badly pronounced. 'Did you ever meet the Jordans?'

'No, not me. But Ellen knew 'un quite well. It's surprising what you can learn about people when you go out cleaning. For a start you can tell by the state of their homes what they're like, not that Ellen would snoop or anything. And if the people are home you wouldn't believe how some of them carry on, as if you're not there, as if you haven't got two good ears clamped to the side of your head. Discussions about money all the time when the two of them were there, Ellen told me.

'The girl were all right, though, she'd have been about fourteen or fifteen at the time. Some fancy name she had. Marina, was it?'

'Miranda.'

Doreen nodded and reached for another slice of heavy cake. She had bitten into it before what Rose had said sank in. 'Then you must know them.'

'No, not really, but I teach their nephew, Joel.'

'They'm rich, too, the Penhaligons. My Cyril tried for years to get work, but he only knew mining, and that was in his blood. I'm sure that's why he's always digging his damn garden, still trying to get back underground, if you ask me. What was I saying? Yes, Cyril. Ellen mentioned his predicament to Louisa Jordan and she said she'd have a word with her brother. Cyril had a long chat with Roger Penhaligon but decided against going to work on one of his holiday campsites. The hours weren't long enough, he said, but to be honest, I think by then he'd just lost heart. The Penhaligons've got a few bob, too, by all accounts.

Ellen did a few stints for them when their own cleaner was off sick and she said, for rich people, they were quite normal. Good job Ellen's got a car, gadding about the way she does.' Doreen thought nothing of the distances she had travelled in her own car over the years to tidy up after people who lived in isolated areas. She chewed thoughtfully and brushed some crumbs from her large bosom which was encased in pastel pink acrylic. 'I did hear that the Jordans had moved away but I can't imagine folk like that lasting up on Bodmin Moor.'

'The husband and daughter didn't go, only Louisa and her sister.'

'So the sister joined her, did she? It was said that Frank Jordan couldn't say no to no woman,' she added enigmatically.

Double negatives aside, the information was useful and provided an obvious explanation for what had seemed mysterious. Petra Penhaligon had said much the same thing, that another woman was involved. Rather than have it known that he had gone off with someone else, or maybe to save his wife's embarrassment, he had used the move to cover his actions. If the woman was married neither of them might wish to be found. But that doesn't explain Miranda, Rose realised. Unless, contrary to what the Penhaligons believed, the girl had sided with her father and gone to live with him as Louisa had suggested to her brother. Instinct told Rose this was not the case.

'You're looking a bit brighter now. Nothing like coffee and cake and a bit of a natter to set you up, that's what I always say.'

And for once Doreen seemed right. Discussing the Jordan/Penhaligon family had taken her mind off what had kept her awake all night.

Doreen got up to go. 'There's a load of veg in there, girl. If you can't use it all pass some on to Laura.'

'Please thank Cyril for me and tell him none of it'll be wasted.' Laura would certainly benefit and it was a fair exchange because Trevor kept her supplied with fish. The barter system was still strong in Cornwall.

When Doreen had gone Rose put the vegetables in the larder which led off the kitchen. It was cool and airy and a handy place for storage and somewhere to keep the freezer.

The cloud began to break up and drift away. The ground would be damp but it was possible to work outside now because the light was good. Rose toyed with the idea of going to the Tate in St Ives. Whoever was being exhibited, the building alone was always worth a visit. From inside, the concave glass semicircle which formed the front reflected the golden sands and the sea, and there was always a Hepworth sculpture worth viewing. And I occasionally get to meet another artist, she thought. But in the end she decided to drive to Zennor again. More work was needed on the painting she had started only yesterday but which seemed like a lifetime ago. Her treat would have to wait.

Being a Saturday there were a few people around but not enough to distract her, not that there was anything from which to distract her except her thoughts. She stared, unseeing, at the canvas and relived the previous evening.

Jack had arrived at the Mount's Bay Inn ahead of her. He sat on the padded bench near the fire, one arm stretched along the length of its back. As Rose pushed open the door he had smiled and stood to buy her a drink.

Longing to talk about Joel and his connection with the sisters, she'd decided to wait. Such coincidences were not rare in Cornwall. Many locals were interrelated with families up and down the county. But two of this family seemed to be missing.

Rose sighed deeply. The beauty of the scenery was dazzling, more so through the sparkle of tears. The conversation she had hoped to have had not taken place. Not wishing to blunder in with her story first Rose had asked, 'What was it you wanted to tell me, Jack?'

'It's about last night. You know, after I left you I said I was meeting some friends.'

'Ah, your CID chums. I bet it was a good evening.' She had actually smiled.

'Yes, but not in the way I intended. They couldn't make it. Something big cropped up in Plymouth. They'd tried to get me at home during the day but I was out with you. Anyway, they caught me at the pub on my mobile.'

Rose had had no idea what was coming. In retrospect it should have been obvious, but she hadn't spotted it, hadn't wanted to, perhaps.

'A woman came in. Alone. We were both at the bar so we got talking. She was meeting a friend. The friend turned up eventually, about half an hour late.'

Rose's mouth had gone dry, there was lead in her stomach.

'I'm taking her out tomorrow,' Jack had said without embarrassment, without guilt.

Rose had nodded. Unexpected jealousy had made her

speechless. She knew how unfair she was being, hadn't she once arranged to meet Jack in a pub in Marazion where she had put an end to their affair? Not that it had ended completely, not until that minute last night.

'I wanted to tell you face to face. You know what it's like down here, we'd have been seen, maybe even by you. I didn't want to go around feeling, wrongly, I was doing something underhand. I wanted you to hear it from me, Rose.'

So she isn't married if it isn't underhand, Rose had realised. 'Where are you taking her?' she had asked stupidly, as if it made any difference. But people in such situations have masochistic tendencies.

'The Newlyn Laundry restaurant, and maybe a drink afterwards.' Jack had paused, wondering how much to tell Rose. 'Her name's Anna Hicks. She's a beautician and runs her own business. Anyway, enough of that. What did you want to see me about?'

'It doesn't matter, it wasn't important. I have to go now, I'm expecting a phone call.' A feeble excuse but the best she could think of at the time.

Rose's fingers were stiff. She had been gripping the paintbrush, which had yet to receive any paint. Gazing out to sea, nothing had changed. The blues and greens shimmered in the winter sunshine, just as they always would, heedless of her pain, or anyone else's pain. Far away seagulls floated on the swell, one or other of them taking off and landing again.

Anna Hicks. Cornish then, or had been married to a Cornishman to possess such a name. A beautician. Rose pictured a slender figure in a crisp white uniform, bare, suntanned legs beneath it. She would have perfect make-up, hair and nails. Someone young, someone beautiful, someone who would not turn Jack away. And bright, too, if she ran a successful business.

Why do I care? she asked herself not for the first time. Why does this hurt so much? I've had my chance. Even up to Thursday I had my chance. Jack wanted more from the relationship than I did. You will not cry, Rose Trevelyan. You will not sodding well cry.

But she did. Only briefly, but it brought relief.

Then she flexed her fingers, picked up the brush and began to work, changing the actual gentle swell to angry waves with forceful strokes of the sable.

By the following Thursday there was still no news of Frank and no one had been in touch with Louisa and Wendy regarding his whereabouts. They had decided to forget the matter.

They were still discussing how they wanted Rose Trevelyan to portray them half an hour before she arrived. 'Two aristocratic-looking ladies?' Louisa suggested with a grin. 'Or two rather intellectual women, struggling against all odds out on the moors?'

'How about two middle-aged women with a streak of vanity?' Wendy was preparing the coffee tray.

'You have no romance, my dear. That's far too realistic.' Louisa opened the window. Her face was hot. Wendy had been baking and the range was fired up. It was a muggy day with a hint of dampness in the air. Christmas was drawing nearer. It had been predicted to be a mild one. 'She's here. I heard the car.'

Louisa went to let Rose in, surprised at the informality of her clothes. I suppose she needs to feel comfortable to work, she realised, taking in the paint-stained jeans, the baggy sweater and the tiredness in her face. 'Coffee first?'

'That would be lovely.' Rose followed her into the cheerful lounge and placed her canvas bag on the thick carpet. When Louisa left the room she went to the tall windows at the back. There was nothing to see but the moors stretching into the distance. No houses, no people, only peace. Barren and wild it might be but Rose could never have lived there, or anywhere where the sea was not in sight.

The sisters appeared together. Coffee was served and they sat down.

Rose took a sip. It was as good as the last time. 'Have you come to any decisions?'

'More or less. Profile, or three-quarter face. Both of us looking in the same direction. Not too formal, not too casual.' It was Wendy who replied.

'That sounds fine. Do you want a plain background or to be posed in front of something in particular?'

'Plain, don't you think?'

Louisa nodded and took a biscuit.

'Shall we get started?' Rose said a few minutes later.

For the next couple of hours she worked without speaking, other than to instruct the women how to sit or stand or hold their heads. She photographed them from every angle then sketched them together, facing one way then the other. Wendy, the shorter of the two, was on her sister's right. The discrepancy in height gave better balance to the portrait Rose had in mind.

It was almost twelve when she packed up her gear. By the look of her clients they were as exhausted as Rose was. 'You have a lovely house,' she said by way of conversation.

'Thank you. We think so, too. Would you like me to show you around?'

'I'd love it, Mrs Jordan.'

'I think first names are called for if we're to see a lot of each other. Follow me.'

Rose put down her bag and climbed the beautiful staircase. It was lined with paintings, all tastefully framed and hung with care. Off the landing there were three bedrooms and, she was glad to see, a proper bathroom. Roughing it without electricity was one thing, lack of washing facilities was another. Each of the rooms was as tasteful as the lounge. Because of Jack she had forgotten to wonder about the family but now it all came back to her. Three bedrooms, two occupied, the third patently not. It contained a bed and furniture but nothing more. Ready for a guest, yes, but Miranda Jordan did not inhabit that room.

The kitchen was amazing, made more so by the smell of baking and the assortment of cookery utensils.

'There's a sort of storeroom,' Louisa said as she opened a door. 'We still haven't finally sorted everything out. You know how it is, if you don't do it all as soon as you move, it never gets done.'

'I've got a similar room so I know what you mean.'

The dining-room was formal and not very interesting and ended the tour.

'You're very lucky,' Rose said as she pulled on her coat. 'I'll see you next week at the same time.'

As she drove back to Newlyn Rose wondered what it was that had struck her as odd, as out of place. Not the empty room, not the women themselves. She was becoming used to their manner. She shook her head. 'Forget it and it'll come back to you,' she told herself.

But it didn't. Not that day.

Reaching home she wondered if it was worth hanging out the washing. There was no sign of rain. She did so, then watched with satisfaction as the cotton sheets and towels snapped in the salty breeze.

Taking an apple and a mug of coffee with her she went up to the attic. One corner had been partitioned off to form a darkroom. She developed two rolls of film and hung the negatives up to dry. Then she studied the sketches she had made. They look a bit too serious, she decided, but knew that with time they would relax, would become accustomed to being scrutinised and studied.

The telephone was ringing. It was Laura. Rose had been half avoiding her. She would know at a glance that something was wrong. 'How are you?'

'Fully recovered. But I feel I've been housebound for weeks. Fancy a drink tonight?'

'Sounds good. Where were you thinking of going?'

'How about the Laundry wine bar for a change?'

'No.'

'Rose?'

'Sorry. I, uh, I . . . oh, God.' And before she could stop herself she was telling Laura about Jack.

'Good for him,' Laura said with far less sympathy than Rose had hoped for. 'Look, you've led him a dance for a couple of years now, what else do you expect. He'd have married you, Rose, given the chance.'

'I know that, Laura. It doesn't make it any easier.'

'Okay, we'll talk about it later. Look, why don't we get a bus somewhere? Marazion or Porthleven. Somewhere we won't run into them. We could eat out ourselves if you like.' It was hardly likely Jack would take the woman to the same place twice within a space of six days but Rose was upset and needed humouring. And Rose was her friend, she hadn't meant to make matters worse.

'I do like. What time shall we meet?' The arrangements made, Rose hung up. She stayed where she was, picturing Jack and the young, nubile Anna Hicks enjoying their meal. To an outsider the name of the restaurant might sound strange but the building had housed a laundry for as long as most people could remember. It had been converted, one part the wine bar, all white and chrome with square candles with four wicks on each table. There were three pyramids of Daz boxes high on shelves, an in-joke to locals. Behind the bar was the restaurant, decorated in the same minimalistic style. Rose wasn't sure whether it made it better or worse that she had been to the place where Jack had also taken his . . . what? Date? Girlfriend? Soon-to-be mistress? No. Floozie, she decided, then burst out laughing. It was a good feeling.

CHAPTER SEVEN

On Saturday evening Barry Rowe sat at the table anticipating with pleasure whatever it was that Rose had decided to cook for him. Cooking was another of her talents.

The first serious storm of the winter was building up, later in the year than usual and promising to be fierce. From the warmth and comfort of the kitchen they listened to the wind. Nothing could be heard over its constant shrieks. Through the window, even in the darkness, they saw the shrubs bend and sway. The sea had lost the myriad colours of daylight and had become a black, threatening terror as it surged forcefully to the shore and crashed against anything that was in its way. The local news had warned that the Promenade was awash and already closed to traffic.

'It won't be long,' Rose said as she turned from the window and lit the gas beneath the vegetables. 'What is it?' she asked, aware that Barry had been watching her.

He picked up a fork and twirled it between his fingers. 'You tell me, Rosie, you're the one who's hardly speaking. You should've cancelled if you don't feel well.'

'I'm fine.'

'But?'

He doesn't know, she realised, word hasn't spread as quickly as I thought it would. It was a week yesterday since Jack had broken the news and she had not heard from him since. Will Barry gloat? she wondered as she joined him at the table. 'Jack's found himself a girlfriend,' she said, without preamble.

'The bastard.'

It was not the reaction she had expected any more than her own had been when she learnt of the existence of Anna Hicks. Barry's anger was genuine, on her behalf, and she loved him the more for it. 'Well, we hadn't been together properly for some time really.'

'Don't defend him, Rose.'

'I wasn't intending to. Anyway, now you know. Let's eat.'

She served the mushroom soup she had made earlier and soft rolls from the local baker's.

'How's the portrait going?' Barry asked when half of his soup had been drunk. He would think about Jack later.

'So far, so good, although I've barely started. We're agreed on how the finished article should look.'

'What're they like, these spinsters?'

'Sisters, not spinsters. One of them was married.' And before she could stop herself she was telling Barry all she knew.

'So the boy who persuaded you to butter up his father for him is their nephew. It seems odd them denying, what, at least four relatives, including the daughter.'

'Well, they certainly are related. When I developed the roll of film I took I could see the distinct likeness between Joel and his Aunt Wendy I knew she reminded me of someone the first time I went there. And, of course, there's this Frank Jordan thing.'

'Rose.' Barry's voice was stern.

She laughed. 'Don't look at me like that.'

'Like what?'

'Over the top of your glasses like a martinet schoolmaster.'

'It's because I worry about you. Especially now with Jack no longer on the scene to keep you in check. You'll only get involved in something that is none of your business and find you're out of your depth and *he* won't be around to bail you out.'

'Then I'll just have to rely on you. And *he* didn't keep me in check, as you call it. Besides, Jack is irrelevant because Joel's father asked me to find out what I could. I liked the man and if I can help, I will.

'But you have to admit, it's a peculiar situation.' Rose stood to clear away the soup bowls. She drained the vegetables and served the mackerel stuffed with apricots and almonds. Barry's favourite.

For a while they ate in silence. The wind continued to howl and the first splatter of rain hit the windows. Rose was unconcerned. The house, built of Cornish granite, had withstood over a century of battering by the elements. She cooked by gas, the heating was fuelled from the same source and there were plenty of candles should the electricity be cut off again.

'Do you think,' Barry began, picking a small bone from

the side of his mouth, 'that the sisters did away with Frank Jordan just before they moved away and that's the reason they are denying they've any family? Perhaps they don't want anyone to make the connection.'

'That's a bit fanciful, even by my standards. No, Doreen Clarke told me he was a bit of a womaniser. I think the move simply provided the opportunity for them to split up.'

'The daughter, too? Even if she was unhappy at home there was no reason for her to give up her university place.'

Rose shrugged as she speared some broccoli. 'Maybe she'd had enough of it all and changed her mind. It's unlike you to play the devil's advocate.'

Barry smiled. Rose wished he would do so more often. His face altered radically. Gone was the line bisecting his forehead and the careworn expression. He was almost handsome. She suddenly realised what else was different about him: both jacket and shirt were new. It was a sad reflection upon herself that she had not noticed before in view of her nagging about his appearance. 'Let's forget the Jordans. I have to tell you, you look really good tonight. I like the new image.'

'Thank you. I wasn't sure you'd noticed. The fish was truly delicious, Rose. Thank you again.'

She refilled their wine glasses and took the plates away, scraping the bones into the bin. 'I haven't done a pudding but there's cheese or fruit or ice-cream.' Barry rarely ate sweet things so surprised Rose for a third time that evening by choosing the latter.

She opened the larder door. The floor was slate, the walls

granite and there was no heating. All edible foodstuffs had been stored there in the days when the property was first built. But it wasn't the chill, the sudden drop in temperature which made her stop and frown. It was what she was seeing. Old coats and boots, a few bits of junk, two spare chairs and the deep freeze. Perfectly normal, just as it always was, nothing had changed. Perfectly normal for me, Rose thought, realising what had been bothering her on the drive back from Bodmin Moor.

'Vanilla all right?' she called out.

'I take it that means it'll have to be.' Barry knew that, like himself, Rose preferred savoury food. The ice-cream would be left over from some other occasion when she had entertained.

She brought the tub to the kitchen and hacked out a serving with a tablespoon. Licking a finger, she placed the glass dish in front of Barry. 'What you were saying, about my clients – you could be right.'

'Oh?' Barry glanced up. The light made blanks of his glasses, hiding his eyes from Rose.

'Perhaps they did do away with him and took the body with them. Don't grin at me as if I'm mad.'

'Not mad, never that, but it was you accusing me of being fanciful earlier.'

'Okay. Tell me this, then. Why should Louisa Jordan and Wendy Penhaligon have a chest freezer in their larder when they don't have electricity, gas or a generator?'

'Ah, you have me there. Maybe they use it for storage. Not for a body, though. They've been there for more than a year, they couldn't have lived with the stench.'

'No, but they could've used it to transport him then buried him somewhere on the moors.'

'I see. So not only did they take the risk of the removal men lifting the lid, these women you could hardly describe as young then went out wielding spades or shovels and dug him a grave in the wilderness. It's as well Jack . . . Hell, I'm sorry, Rose. I didn't mean to bring up his name again.'

'It's all right. It isn't something we can avoid. Besides, Laura said I had it coming to me.'

'Did she?' It surprised Barry how candid women friends could be with one another, but as he had never had any close friends himself he was unsure whether the same applied to men. 'I don't feel happy about you going up there. I mean, if there's the slightest basis of truth in your suspicions you could be in danger.'

'My suspicions? It was you who first voiced them. Besides, you'll know I'm there on Thursday mornings.'

'Quite. But if you didn't come back one day, it'd be too late to help you.'

'Now who's crazy? I can't give up this commission. The money's more than good but I've also got to think of my reputation. It could lead to more work. It certainly won't if I let them down.'

'Not if they've cut themselves off so drastically.'

Rose considered what Barry had said and wondered anew exactly why the sisters wanted their portrait painted.

The telephone interrupted her thoughts. It sounded tinny and distant over the noise of the storm which had increased in force, building itself up for the small hours when it would blow itself out with the turn of the tide. 'Put the coffee on, would you? I won't be a minute.'

Rose crossed the hallway and went into the sitting room. The telephone was on a small table behind the door, facing the window. Through the rain she could just make out the mountainous waves and the high spumes of spray which had rendered the Promenade impassable. 'Hello,' she said cheerfully, expecting it to be her mother.

'Hello, Rose.'

She swallowed, wondering at the tightness in her chest. 'What do you want, Jack?'

'I just called to see how you are, if you've escaped the flu. That's what friends do.'

His words made her feel vulnerable and a little ashamed. It had been her suggestion they remained friends, Jack was now simply acting upon it. And she had rarely hesitated before telephoning him even after their initial affair had ended. 'I'm fine, thank you, although Laura's been pretty rough.' Laura's brother had been to school with Jack.

'I know. I called in to see her the other day. Didn't she mention it?'

'She might have done.' Rose knew she hadn't. 'How did it go, your date with Anna?'

'Great. We got on really well.'

Meaning what? Rose thought. Great company? Great in bed? Great food? It was unlike Jack to be enigmatic. 'Good luck, then. I have to go, I've got someone here for dinner.'

'Barry Rowe?' he asked, making Rose wish she could come out with the name of a man he'd never heard of.

'Yes. Look, Jack, was there something particular you wanted to discuss?'

'No. Like I said, this was just a friendly call and it's been over a week since we've spoken.'

'Keep in touch. I must go. Bye.' With a shaking hand she replaced the receiver. It would be good to be out in the storm, to let the wind and the rain cool her burning face. But Barry was waiting. 'Before you ask, that was Jack,' she told him.

'You didn't talk long.'

'There was nothing to say.'

The coffee was still filtering through the machine, making soothing plopping sounds. A sudden crash made them both jump.

'It's the shed.' Barry was on his feet and out of the door before Rose began to move. She ran after him, pulling the kitchen door inwards against the wind, straining her muscles as the rain swept towards her.

Barry coat flying, rain plastering his shirt to his body and his thinning hair to his head, yanked at the shed door and managed to get it closed despite one of the hinges having been damaged. He pad-locked it shut and ran for the house.

'Thanks. I meant to lock it earlier.' There was nothing in there of value but the door had a tendency to fly open in strong winds. 'Give me your jacket and go and sit by the fire. I'll bring the coffee in.' She laid a tray; adding a bottle of brandy and two glasses. 'You can't walk home in this. Wait until you're dry then order a taxi.' The window panes rattled and sudden draughts blew smoke back down the chimney. Now and then the logs hissed as moisture found its way into the fireplace. 'God, listen to it.' She hoped the fishermen who were out were beyond the storm. There would be a lot of damage done before morning.

Barry's cab arrived at eleven. Rose wondered how he could bear to return to his awful flat over the shop. It was cramped and in need of decoration and he cared little for furniture as long as he had enough for his use. But it was his choice and he seemed content.

Rose decided to clear up rather than leave the task for the morning. She needed to think, about Jack and about Louisa Jordan and what had become of her husband. She could not back out of the job, not now. Maybe, she decided as she put out the light, I'll finish the portrait without saying anything.

Miranda lay on her bed listening to music. The piano concerto she normally enjoyed sounded harsh to her ears. She got up and turned off the CD player. It wouldn't be long before she would be going home. The flat was furnished. Everything she owned would fit into the second-hand car she had purchased a few months previously. She and Michael had come to an agreement. Miranda would go back and assess where she stood and, if everything worked out, he would visit her after Christmas. 'The situation at home isn't right,' she had explained. 'I need time. I'll ring you each day I promise.' But she had refused to give him a contact number, not that she knew it. Michael had concurred because he couldn't force himself upon her family not when she wasn't certain she'd be welcome herself. She had disappointed her mother and her aunt when she'd taken off for London and not told them where she would be living.

It had not been easy cutting all the ties. It wasn't a case of forgiving her mother or hating her for what she had done. She had left to protect her. If she wasn't around and no one knew where to find her, no one could ask any questions. And what had happened had made university become of secondary importance. If it all came out no one would have employed her anyway, degree or not. But she had begun to wonder if her fears had been justified.

She had dropped the name Jordan. In London she was known as Miranda Penhaligon, a name rightfully hers as she had been registered at birth as Miranda Penhaligon-Jordan. Her mother was proud to be Cornish and had wished her daughter to retain the name.

Rain pattered against the window. London rain which left the glass smeared; not with salt but with smuts and grease. She leant her head against the pane and watched the traffic in the street below. Tail-lights showed as red streaks on the wet tarmac and water from the building opposite dripped from faulty guttering on to an awning below.

But there's no salt spray on Bodmin Moor, she thought, reminding herself once more that her mother had moved, because all her memories were of Penzance and she had never been to the new place.

She ran a hand through the tangle of fair curls. I'll just turn up, she decided. I won't write. If they turn me away it's no more than I deserve. She smiled wanly, aware of her London image. They might not even recognise me, she realised. After all, it had been quite a long time.

Something good had come of it though, she thought. If

I hadn't come here I would never have met Michael. But if he ever discovered the reason she had left she would surely lose him.

Joel Penhaligon was doubly grateful to Rose Trevelyan. His father's attitude towards him seemed to have changed, although Joel realised he might be seeing him differently now, and therefore his own attitude had also altered.

On Saturday night, prior to meeting some friends, he sat down to eat with his parents.

'Did Rose say anything to you on Wednesday evening, about your aunts?' Roger took a sip of his after-dinner whisky.

'No, she didn't, actually. Not that there was much chance. Someone else wanted to speak to her after the class was over. It was strange, her meeting them by chance like that.'

'Chance? There's no such thing. Fate, maybe, that's a different matter. It may even have been deliberate on their part.'

Petra watched the interaction between her husband and son and was glad that the tension between them no longer existed. In fairness, it had mostly been on Joel's side. Now his future was settled he was much more pleasant to both of them. But it was odd, about Roger's sisters. She had never found them easy to get on with, especially Wendy, whom Joel resembled physically, but she still missed Miranda who had been like the daughter she had always wanted. Frank Jordan had been nothing more than an arrogant bore.

'Did Miranda ever hint that things weren't right at

home? You two were very close despite the difference in your ages.'

'No, she never said a word. Only that she was sorry to be leaving but as she was going to university anyway it wouldn't be quite such a blow.'

'I don't know. There's something behind all this, Petra. I mean, especially now with someone trying to track down Frank. I know he owes me money and that he wasn't as discreet as he might have been when it came to other women, but it makes me wonder if he was involved in something worse. It wouldn't surprise me.'

'Only one thing about that man surprises me, and that was putting the house in Louisa's name.'

'You have it there. Perhaps he was in more financial trouble than we knew and wanted to ensure he had a roof over his head. If the bailiffs were sent in they couldn't take it away from her. A wife isn't responsible for her husband's debts.'

'What exactly did Uncle Frank do?'

'No one is certain, Joel. He had the financial services business but that couldn't possibly have paid for the lifestyle he led. Shady dealings, I expect. That could explain why solicitors are trying to find him. We've all assumed it would be good news, a legacy or something. Perhaps he owes money elsewhere.'

'I still don't understand about Miranda, Dad. No matter what Aunt Louisa said, she'd never have gone off with her father.'

'I know that, son, that's why I contacted the police in the first place. But she was of age so there wasn't much they could do about it.

'When you see Rose on Wednesday ask her to give me a ring.' She would have seen his sisters again by now but he didn't want to bother her unduly

Petra poured coffee. 'Do you really have to go out tonight?' she asked Joel as she frowned at the window. The bare branches of the trees were bent almost double now and the rain lashed down, noisy and relentless. There would be a mess to clear up in the morning.

'He's seventeen, Petra, and it's Saturday night. Of course he has to go out.'

Joel grinned. He was beginning to understand his father a little better. Once he would have taken the comment as sarcasm, now he realised that it arose from a dry sense of humour.

CHAPTER EIGHT

Inspector Jack Pearce was in an introspective mood, which was unusual. There were no current uncertainties where work was concerned, he got on with the job as best he could with the information available. Women were a different matter. What seemed to be information, a known fact about their character, often turned out to be nothing more than a particular mood. And he couldn't fathom Rose's present one or if it was to do with Anna Hicks.

Anna was good-looking, fun to be with and an easy conversationalist but the relationship was only just over a week old. Jack knew better than to believe it would not change.

But he was worried. When he had arrived at Camborne police station that morning he was told that Roger Penhaligon had been on the telephone. 'I know we went through all this before,' he had told the officer to whom he had spoken, 'but it seems solicitors are advertising for my brother-in-law to come forward. It's more than a year now and we haven't heard a word and, more importantly, neither has his daughter, Miranda, contacted us. I really feel this needs looking into more thoroughly.' There was probably nothing more to it than a family feud or rivalry but alarm bells had rung when he learnt that Penhaligon's last words had been, 'We know where my sisters are now, thanks to Joel's art tutor, Rose Trevelyan. She not only teaches my son, she's painting my sisters' portraits.'

'She never said a bloody word,' Jack muttered. 'She met me in the pub that night and never mentioned a word of any of this.' He sighed. Of course she hadn't. She had said there was something she had wanted to discuss with him but he had dropped his bombshell first and Rose had made an excuse to leave early.

Monday evening had arrived. Jack sat in his ground-floor flat in Morrab Road nursing a small whisky, pen and paper to hand. The road outside ran down to the sea and was lined with sturdy properties, some of which had been converted into premises for professional people. Others catered for bed and breakfast and many of the remaining houses had been divided into flats.

There was certainly something going on in the Jordan/Penhaligon family but it might all be innocent. A week or so ago he could have discussed it with Rose, now he wasn't certain what his reception would be. It was all very well her saying she wanted friendship but he had seen the expression on her face when he had told her about Anna. He had to admit it had pleased him to recognise it as jealousy.

Without realising it he had been making a list. He looked down and read it.

Frank Jordan does a bunk.
Roger Penhaligon reports his niece missing.

No police action is taken.
At the same time Louisa Jordan moves to Bodmin Moor, closely followed by her sister, Wendy Penhaligon.
Solicitors try to trace Frank Jordan.
Penhaligon gets in touch again.
Rose Trevelyan discovers relationship between the two families. She's the link between the family members who have not disappeared.

'She would be, damn her. She already knows more than we do.' The second sigh was deeper. He had no option but to speak to her. Face to face. But if he rang in advance she might come up with an excuse not to see him.

No, he decided, this wasn't really a case, no crime had been committed. Miranda Jordan had been of age and her mother had been unconcerned, her father had run off with a bimbo and now an ancient relative had left him a few hundred quid, it was as simple as that. But it was still an excuse to see Rose. And if she was taking an active interest there might be something in it. 'That woman's curiosity is boundless,' he said, talking to himself as he often did when alone.

He drove over to Newlyn and pulled into her drive. Rose's car was there and a dim light showed through the kitchen window. It was the hall light, set on a timer, the one Jack had persuaded her to purchase and he had installed. He rapped on the door, sensing already that Rose wasn't in. He went home and left a telephone message.

To his surprise and anger she returned none of his calls until Thursday evening. Meanwhile he forgot Frank Jordan and got on with more important matters.

On Wednesday he took Anna to the cinema. She was a little subdued but he did not know her well enough to ask what was the matter.

Rose promised Joel she would find out what she could from his aunts, although how she was to go about it was beyond her. Bring up marriage, she thought, talk about David and not having children and see how Louisa reacts to that. Joel's confidence had increased now that he knew where his future lay. He had produced another fine drawing.

Rose worked steadily from Sunday until Wednesday when she packed up early because of her class. The storm had broken by Sunday morning and she had taken advantage of the bright blue sky and gone out to photograph its violent effects. The Zennor painting was near completion and she had sketched in the background to the portrait, outlining the position of the two figures. Soon the really serious part would begin.

Thursday morning dawned dry and sunny. December had arrived but it seemed more like April. Rose set off knowing that she would not be able to remain silent, that she would have to say something to draw the sisters out.

She pulled up outside the house, surprised to see a second car to the side of it. No one had anticipated her arrival this time, the door remained closed as she approached it. She banged the iron knocker against the wood. There was a shout from inside, two words which she could not make out. The door opened and Louisa, red-faced, appeared. 'Mrs Trevelyan, my sincere apologies, we tried to reach you at home before you left but we were obviously too late. I expect you carry a mobile phone but we didn't have the number.

'Look, this is highly embarrassing, but we've changed our minds about the portrait. It's no reflection upon you, I promise, and, naturally, we'll settle the whole bill as soon as you send it. I can't say how sorry we are for wasting your time. Something entirely unexpected has cropped up. I really can't explain, but that's the way things must be.'

Rose knew she must look an idiot. She was standing totally still, her hand clutching the strap of her canvas bag, her mouth open. She was unable to find a single thing to say. They know, was all she could think, they know I'm in touch with their brother and his family. There is definitely something going on here they don't want me to find out.

'Mrs Trevelyan?'

'Sorry. I'm surprised, that's all. Everything seemed to be going so well. However, it has to be your decision. I'll send you a bill, but I can't possibly charge you the full amount.'

'I insist. We have put you to so much inconvenience and you might have missed other commissions. I'm sorry we can't even invite you in for coffee. We're in a bit of a fix at the moment.'

'I understand.' I understand nothing, she thought. Not yet, but I will. 'It's all right. I'll, um, well, I'll make my way back then.'

'I can't thank you enough for the way in which you have taken this. Maybe some other time.' She paused. 'Anyway, please invoice us immediately.'

Rose nodded and turned away. Whatever had cropped up must have been very recent for them not to have left a message on the answering-machine last night. And it has to be to do with the daughter or the husband, she realised as she began the drive home. I'll ring Roger and let him know. He might have heard something himself by now.

At home she got the canvas out of her satchel and stared at it. It really belonged to Louisa and Wendy, they would be paying for it. Later she would decide what to do about it.

At six she dialled the Penhaligons' number. Roger was at home.

'This looks more peculiar by the minute. I spoke to the police again this morning, but I don't think they took me very seriously Damn nuisance. Still, I'm relying on you to dig around a bit. Good job you didn't leave that canvas there this morning, you've got an excuse for one more visit. I hope it's too big to put in the post.'

'Yes, it is.' Rose was thinking, chewing the end of her hair as she did so. It was a childhood habit which had never left her. I'll do it, she decided. I'll go back there again. And then another thought struck her. 'Look, I know an inspector in the D & C Police. Perhaps if I have a word with him?' She left the question hanging, hoping that he would say it wasn't worth it. Roger had told her he'd spoken to a constable.

'Would you? We'd be so grateful. You seem to have done a lot for us already Rose. Joel's a different boy lately.'

'I'm glad. I'll be in touch.' She rang Jack immediately knowing that if she hesitated she would change her mind.

'I was beginning to think you'd emigrated,' he said, trying to make light of her neglect of his calls.

'Sorry I've been a bit busy. Jack, there's something

104

I'd like to talk to you about. Are you free some time this week?' Once, she would not have needed to ask, he'd have volunteered to come immediately and therefore his answer surprised her.

'How about in fifteen minutes? If you're not busy that is.' How cagey they were being.

Now that the arrangement was made Rose felt nervous. Have I time to change, to brush my hair and put some make-up on? she wondered. No, I never bothered before unless we were going out or he was coming for dinner. It would appear too obvious if she did so now.

Although until recently he had been a frequent visitor to the house it made her stomach lurch when his large frame was silhouetted in the kitchen window. Rose let him in, glancing quickly at his dark, handsome looks then moving away afraid of the frisson which still existed between them, at least on her side, anyway

'How's things?' Jack was as unsure as his hostess as to how he was supposed to act.

'I'm not totally sure. Would you like a drink?'

'Just a small one. I've got the car.'

Rose fumbled with the corkscrew. It slid off the plastic seal as she tried to break it with the point. Jack reached out a hand. 'Here, let me do it.' His fingers briefly touched hers. She could feel the heat of his body and smell his familiar smell, a mixture of clean cotton and aftershave. The cork slid out smoothly and he poured the wine. 'Now, what did you want to talk to me about?' He guessed it would be to do with the phone call Roger Penhaligon had made to the station earlier and that he might actually glean some hard facts. As she spoke he listened carefully his chin resting in the palm of his hand. 'How much?' His hand fell into his lap when Rose mentioned the sum of money the sisters had agreed to pay her. 'God, and you haven't even finished the portrait.'

'I know. And I still don't understand why they commissioned me in the first place. I mean, if they've got a problem I could always have gone back another time to complete the work.'

'This other car, did you notice the registration number?'

'No. I was so stunned I didn't think about it. But it wasn't a new car.'

'Never mind.' He chewed his firm lower lip. 'The thing is, Rose, I just don't see what I can do. No one's broken the law as far as I'm concerned. All right, two people are missing and these seemingly whacky sisters have changed their minds which is odd, but no more than that.'

Rose took a sip of her wine. It was as she had expected. Jack's hands were tied. Now there was nothing more to say 'Well, thank you for coming, anyway.'

'Is that it? I'm being dismissed? I'd help if I could, you know that.'

'No problem. I'm going to see them one more time. I might find out something useful.'

'Rose, you really shouldn't . . .'

'Really shouldn't what, Jack?'

'Nothing. Forget it.'

'Look, you'd better leave. Anna might not like you coming here.' She was aware she sounded like a jealous teenager and she certainly hadn't intended mentioning Anna's name.

Jack's blue eyes widened. This wasn't like Rose. 'Why should she mind? She knows we're old friends. Besides, she isn't that sort of person.'

Old friends. It sounded like an insult. Perhaps that's how Barry felt when she referred to him in that way. 'I see. So you've discussed me with her.'

'No, not discussed. I happened to mention that you were an artist, a good one, and that I'd known you for several years. I've only seen the woman a couple of times, I haven't spelt out everything about us.'

Rose sniffed and topped up her glass, ignoring Jack's empty one. It was ironical that she now felt more insulted that he had not discussed her with Anna. 'What's she like?' She hated herself for asking.

'In what way?'

Rose looked up. There was a hint of laughter in his eyes. 'As a person.' Go on, torture yourself, she thought.

'Cheerful, witty and pleasant company is my first impression. Like myself, typical Cornish looks. Long dark hair, curvy figure, a little taller than you are. Satisfied, or is there anything else you'd like to know?' He was smiling openly now. 'Oh, and she's forty-three.'

Dark, curvy and forty-three. Not at all the blonde floozie Rose had imagined. 'No. I was just curious.'

'And we all know where that's got you before.'

'Don't start, Jack, I'm not in the mood for a row.'

'Start? It was merely a truthful observation. Look, just for once, Rose, take my advice and stay out of this family affair. Whatever's going on, whatever help you give them, they'll end up resenting you if you interfere.'

'What on earth makes you think you're any longer in a position to give me advice?'

Jack was on his feet and had already opened the door. He turned to face her. 'Because I'm still your friend. You seem to have a very selective memory, my dear. It was you who broke off our relationship, after which you saw other men. You seem to resent the opposite applying.'

'Saw, yes. The odd drink or dinner, nothing more than that,' she added defiantly. Rose felt her face redden.

'And then you led me to believe you were interested again but really you were keeping me on a string. I'm sorry if my seeing Anna upsets you, but that's the way it is.' Jack was furious. A month or so ago, just when he thought he had another chance with Rose, she had become offhand and found excuses not to see him. Well, she couldn't have it both ways. 'I'd have married you, you know that, and I'd have been a faithful husband. But you didn't want me. Therefore you have no right, no right whatsoever, to treat me like this. I am perfectly free to see anybody I like, as are you. Goodnight, Rose.' He closed the door with quiet deliberation and walked down the drive to his car.

Rose stared at the space where he had stood and knew she had lost something important. She knew, too, that it was entirely her own fault.

Almost in defiance she poured the rest of the wine. Food would have to wait, she had no appetite now. Forget him, she told herself, forget the man even exists. But she could still smell his aftershave.

Later, she poached a couple of eggs, ate only one of them then washed up and went to bed where sleep came

108

more easily than she had imagined it would.

Although Friday dawned sunny and mild Rose stayed close to the house. She cleaned and ironed and planned her next set of watercolours for Barry Rowe. It was another discipline, one she didn't want to lose.

At four forty just as darkness began to descend over the bay she pulled on a thick jacket against the easterly wind and walked down to Newlyn. Because of the suitable tides and weather there were few fishing-boats in the harbour although several masts stood out against the skyline. The tower of St Mary's church in Penzance was outlined blackly against the purple clouds, a landmark almost as prominent as that of St Michael's Mount. Beyond it fields stretched upwards into the distance.

She shopped in the Co-op, which stayed open until 11 p.m. Picking up a few basic things she needed, she decided to have a drink. Her own company had begun to pall. She needed to be amongst people, to talk to the fishermen or their women about subjects unrelated to missing people or Detective Inspector Jack Pearce.

Music flowed from the Swordfish bar next to the Co-op. About to walk in, she heard someone calling her name.

'Fancy a drink?'

Standing outside the Star Inn, no more than a few yards away was Trevor Penrose, Laura's husband. 'Yes. I do. Where's Laura?'

He pushed open the door for her. 'We've had a row.' He grinned. In contrast to his wife he was short and stocky. His brown hair curled over his collar and a tiny gold cross dangled from one ear.

'Another one?' Rose smiled back. Her friends' marriage had always been tempestuous yet they seemed to thrive on it.

'It'll blow over by the time I get back, or she'll have gone to bed. You know how it is.'

'I certainly do,' Rose said as he ordered their drinks.

They remained at the bar where they both felt more comfortable. The wooden boards of the floor were practical. The pub stood opposite the fish market and the men came in in their overalls and boots or the gear they had worn to sea. Both she and Trevor knew all the customers and they spoke to several of them.

'What did you mean, about us rowing?' Trevor asked when the people they were talking to had moved away

'Not you. Me.' Rose found herself telling him about Jack. Trevor was a taciturn man. He said nothing until she had finished.

'Laura told me,' he said. 'Do you care?'

'A bit.' A lot, actually she added silently. A lot more than I thought I would. 'But what I resent is his attitude, the way he still tries to dictate to me.'

Trevor grinned more widely and took a long swig of beer. 'Somebody has to try much good it'll ever do them. You're as pig-headed as Laura. One more drink then I'm off. She'll have cooled down by now. I'll give her a ring to say I'll bring back a Chinese, that should do the trick. You're two of a kind, you know. You and Jack. Neither of you knows what you really want. And he's right, about keeping out of other people's business. No good ever comes of getting involved. You, of all people, should know that.'

Rose watched him walk to the phone. For Trevor that

110

was an extremely long speech. She bought their second drink while he was speaking to Laura and considered what he had said. He was right, she didn't know what she wanted. Not Jack full time, but not him with another woman either. Selfish bitch, she thought.

Twenty minutes later they parted outside the pub. Trevor turned left for the Chinese takeaway and home while Rose made her way along the Strand past The Fradgen and on up the hill, her carrier bag swinging. There was a cargo ship in the bay and a trawler heading for the harbour. She crossed the road to watch it come in through the narrows. Its engine chugged, the sound carrying clearly across the water in the stillness of the early evening. Above, stars glittered and promised a cold night. The quarter moon lay on its side like a pale fingernail clipping. From her high vantage point she could see the whole huge sweep of the bay from Newlyn harbour to the blur in the distance which was the Lizard Point. Along the coastline the clustered lights of the villages twinkled. The huge satellite discs of Goonhilly were now invisible as were the white pointed sails of the wind farm.

It's Saturday tomorrow, she thought. And I know what I'm going to do. And Jack Pearce can do the other thing. And then she remembered. That other car at the farmhouse. It wasn't new and it was small and there had been a teddy bear in a fisherman's jersey dangling from the rear mirror. Not a man's car, then. Miranda, it had to be Miranda's car, and her return had to be more than a coincidence. But what did any of it have to do with the portrait? Rose decided to find out.

* * *

111

Louisa Jordan could not believe her daughter had come home. Every time she looked at her or heard her voice she was filled with joy. What a shock it had been when she had opened the door at eight-thirty on Thursday morning and discovered Miranda standing there. Hearing the knock she had assumed Rose Trevelyan had turned up early for some reason.

For several seconds neither of the women had spoken. There seemed too much to say. 'Oh, Mum.' It was Miranda who broke the silence. It was all she had said, but the pleading note in her voice had been enough. Louisa had embraced her, holding her tightly, aware of the tears running down both their faces.

Wendy had appeared and was equally startled but there had been a coldness between aunt and niece, inexplicable to Louisa who knew Wendy adored Miranda.

Over breakfast Louisa had demanded no explanations and none had been given. That her daughter was home was enough for the moment. Unless Miranda had changed, and she certainly had physically, an explanation would come, she knew her well enough for that. Two days had passed but no questions had been asked on either side. Wendy continued to treat Miranda coolly and was repaid in kind.

'I was working in an insurance office,' Miranda had volunteered on Friday evening. 'I gave a month's notice but I didn't work it all out. I just couldn't wait one more day.' Unable to sleep she had got up and packed and driven down during the lonely early hours of the morning. She had sat outside in the car, waiting until a reasonable time before knocking. 'It was quite a job finding you. Is it all right if I stay for a while?'

'You know you can stay for as long as you like,' Louisa had reassured her. There had been no opportunity for the discussion she wanted to have with her daughter because Wendy always seemed to be hovering in the background. But it could wait. There was a lot they had to tell each other.

'She's exhausted,' Wendy said on Saturday morning. 'And, I believe, worried. You can tell by her face. Let her sleep, we'll do the shopping as usual. We can leave her a note.'

Miranda didn't wake until ten. Still unsure of her unfamiliar surroundings she couldn't immediately think where she was or what had woken her. The door, she realised, someone's knocking at the door. She stepped into her mules, pulled on her dressing gown and knotted the belt as she went downstairs. The house was surprisingly warm despite the lack of facilities, but the fires had been lit and the Cornish range gave out a lot of heat. And, of course, it was milder than it had been in London. Overhead was a blue sky across which floated a few wisps of cloud. There were no buildings here to obscure her view of it.

But on the doorstep stood a petite woman with shoulder-length wavy auburn hair in which a few strands of grey were visible. She wore a smart tan coat, unbuttoned, showing a brown cord skirt and cream sweater beneath it. Under her arm was a large oblong package tied up in strong wrapping-paper.

'Is Louisa in, or Wendy?' Rose asked, showing as little surprise as possible, but aware this lovely girl could only be, as she had guessed, Joel's cousin, Miranda. The family resemblance was strong.

'No, I don't think so. The house is very quiet. You must

113

think I'm stupid, but I've only just woken up.'

Rose took in the mass of fair curls and the dark circles beneath the eyes of the attractive girl. She was no longer in any doubt. As she looked more closely the resemblance to Louisa was unmistakable. 'May I come in for a moment? I've brought this for . . . Louisa.' She had almost said 'your mother' before remembering Louisa had claimed to be childless. No, Rose thought, she said there wasn't anyone else, which was a different matter if they were estranged.

'Forgive me. Of course. I'm dying for a coffee, would you like one?'

'Love one. Thank you.' Rose followed her to the kitchen.

'I'm Miranda, by the way.' She shook the kettle which was simmering on top of the range to ensure it was full and filled the old-fashioned glass percolator, then she reached for the sheet of paper on the table. 'Ah, they've left me a note. My mother and aunt are out but they don't say what time they'll be back, only that they've gone to St Austell to shop.'

Rose nodded. She was safe enough for a while, unless they'd left at the crack of dawn. Miranda had volunteered her name and relationship to the two sisters, what else might Rose learn? For one thing the daughter was less formal than the mother. The coffee was still excellent but was served in two stoneware mugs and drunk at the kitchen table. 'I'm Rose Trevelyan. I was commissioned to paint a portrait of Louisa and Wendy only they've changed their minds. As they've offered to pay me in full I felt they should at least have the canvas with the work I'd started. They own it by rights.'

114

'A portrait?' Miranda laughed. It made her look younger. She shook the mane of hair in disbelief. 'It seems so very out of character. Neither of them is vain.'

There were so many things Rose wanted to ask, about her father, for instance, and where the girl had been, but it was impossible. She was supposed to be a stranger. And anything she said would probably be reported back to Louisa.

'You're obviously an artist, then. I didn't know they mixed in such circles.'

'I teach art, too. In Penzance. But I live in Newlyn.' She had seen her opportunity and would not waste it.

'Penzance?' Miranda's face creased with painful memories.

'You know it?'

'I used to live there. We all did.'

'Do you still have any relatives there?' Louisa had denied their existence, would Miranda do so too?

'None that we keep in touch with.'

'Don't you miss them?'

Miranda shook her head. 'I'll get some more coffee.' She stood and tightened the belt of her dressing gown but Rose had seen the glisten of tears. When she sat down she was composed again.

Miranda decided that she could get to like Rose Trevelyan, she seemed such an easy person to talk to. 'I do miss them,' she admitted, 'but there are reasons why I don't keep in touch. There was some family scandal and my father disappeared. My mother thought it best to sever all ties. I made a new start, but it didn't really work out, I was never happy in London.'

'And now you're back?'

'Yes, now I'm back.'

'The reason I asked about relatives is this. Your face was so familiar to me. One of my students drew someone that if it wasn't you, must be related. His name's Joel Penhaligon.'

Miranda pressed her fingers to her mouth. Her other hand, holding the mug, trembled and concentric circles formed on the top of the coffee. 'Joel's my cousin. How is he?'

'He's fine. He's going to be an artist. I met his parents, too, they're nice people.'

'I know.'

'Miranda?'

They both turned at once. They had not heard the car or the well-oiled front door opening because they were at the back of the house. In the doorway stood Wendy. There were several bags in her hands. Her face was expressionless. 'We didn't expect to see you again, Mrs Trevelyan.'

Rose noted the new formality. 'I brought this.' She indicated the package propped against a cupboard door. 'I was coming this way anyway and as you've been more than generous with payment I felt you ought to have it.'

'There was really no need, but thank you anyway. I see Miranda has played the hostess.'

Miranda, not my niece. Maybe Wendy hoped Rose was none the wiser. Louisa appeared behind her, her brow creased in a frown. The undercurrents were almost palpable. Rose stood and picked up her handbag; she knew she would gain no more by staying and the older women's body language made it clear they wanted her to leave. 'My account's in an envelope in the parcel,' she said. 'Goodbye. And thanks for the coffee, Miranda.'

'Any time.'

I doubt that, Rose thought, although there had been a wistful expression on the girl's face, as though she would have liked to talk for longer about her Penzance relatives. She had not wanted to lose contact, that was obvious, so why had she done so?

Rose signalled and pulled out into the main road. Miranda knows my name and where I live, if she wants to talk to me she can find the number in the phone book. And I strongly suspect she will contact me, she thought as she negotiated a gap in the traffic to overtake a lorry. I think she's desperate to talk to someone. But what a coincidence. Someone advertises for the father and the daughter turns up. Coincidence, or are the two events connected? And should I tell Roger Penhaligon? He'd be relieved to know that Miranda was safe, as would Joel. She need not mention the girl's whereabouts; if they guessed it, the information would not have come from her. On the other hand it might be better to say nothing, to just let the matter drop. It was a family affair and none of her business. She had the drive home in which to think about it carefully. How different the scenery appeared in comparison with that first visit. Beneath the blue sky the various hues of brown were apparent and the greens and yellows stood out clearly against the granite boulders. No longer was the scenery a uniform grey, shrouded in rain. Rose turned on the radio and sang as she drove. Miranda was back, the puzzle might yet be solved. However, the matter was taken out of her hands when Roger Penhaligon telephoned later that day. He almost begged her for information, questioning her at length. Unless she lied there was no other option but to tell him what she knew.

'You've seen her?' Roger was astonished.

'Yes. Will you tell Joel?'

'I'm not sure. I'm not sure what I should do. It all seems such a mess. He hasn't really been the same since she left, he's lost some of his confidence somehow. Perhaps that's why he came to you for help. Anyway, I'll think about it. What I don't want is to upset Joel further. But thanks, anyway. It's a great relief to know nothing's happened to her. Did she tell you where she'd been?'

'Working in London.'

'Not with Frank then.'

'No.'

'Ah, well, maybe he'll reappear suddenly as well.'

Rose doubted it. But she had, against her better judgement, told Roger what he wanted to know and now, surely the rest was up to him.

CHAPTER NINE

Two weeks had passed in which Rose had been busy. The Zennor painting was finished and hanging in Geoff Carter's light and airy gallery. The price sticker he had attached to it showed a figure higher than Rose had anticipated asking. 'You're getting better all the time. Rose,' he had told her. 'Don't sell yourself short.' But she was disappointed she had not been able to complete the double portrait. It had offered a real challenge, one she hoped would be repeated in the future.

There were now only two weeks until Christmas. Since David's death seven years ago any celebrations had always been kept low key. She had stayed with her parents the first year but thereafter, at Rose's insistence, they had gone abroad or on a cruise as had been their habit since their early retirement from farming. Although she received numerous offers from friends she preferred to spend the time in relative solitude. But not this year. Her parents were arriving on the twenty-third and on Christmas Eve she was holding a party. On Christmas Day morning they were going to Laura and Trevor for drinks then home for a late lunch. Barry Rowe would be there to make up the foursome. It would be far more hectic than usual.

Rose sat in the bay of the window tapping a biro against her teeth. She had spent an hour planning the menu and was now wondering whether she had the nerve to invite Jack and Anna for the evening and why she wanted them to be there. To show there were no hard feelings or to meet her rival? she asked herself. More than likely it was a bit of both. She picked up the phone and rang Jack at work. It was the first time she had spoken to him since he had walked out that evening but, typically, he seemed to have forgotten their argument.

'If you're sure you don't mind, then we'll be glad to come,' he answered agreeably.

'Oughtn't you to ask Anna first?'

'We hadn't made any plans and her daughter's still in Australia.'

This was the first Rose had heard of a family. Presumably Anna was divorced, or maybe a single parent. The deed done, her conscience was clear.

Her last class before the break was tomorrow. Now that they knew Miranda was safe Roger may well have made further inquiries of his own. She hoped there would be a chance to speak to Joel in case there was any news. She glanced at her guest list again. There would be quite a crowd to fit in but they would spread themselves between the sitting room and kitchen and they all knew each other. 'I'll start shopping tomorrow,' she said. The deep freeze was now half empty, there would be room for the things she intended to bake.

There were a few bits of paperwork to see to and some files of old negatives to go through. This took until lunchtime when she pulled on her waxed jacket, locked the house and started to walk along the coastline to the popular fishing village of Mousehole. It was another fine day and mild for the time of year. The sea, which could broil and rage in a storm, was flat and calm. Its azure surface sparkled and made Rose squint as she leant against the newly erected wooden fence looking across the bay. She needed ideas for her next canvas. If possible, she did not want to repeat what she, or other artists, had produced before. But the villages running down to the sea, the sandy bays and the barren landscape dotted with disused tin-mines were what people seemed to want. St Michael's Mount itself had been done to death. The Zennor painting had been an inspiration half land, half sea, she needed another idea like that. Morrab Gardens, maybe? In December, without the council-planted flowerbeds, it reverted to its more natural state with only sub-tropical palms and plants. It was worth a try.

She walked on, enjoying the feel of the sun on her head. When she reached the little fishing village she spotted Geoff Carter sitting on one of the seats on the harbour wall watching the boats bobbing on the water.

'Rose,' he said, standing to greet her. 'I thought you'd be out working somewhere on a day like this.'

'I am. I'm thinking.'

'Great, because I may have some good news for you soon.'

'Oh?'

'You'll have to wait, it isn't certain yet.'

Rose studied the tall, lean man with his swept-back hair which grew over his collar. He looked the part of a gallery owner in cord trousers, a checked shirt and body-warmer. He had taken her out to dinner a couple of times. She liked him a lot, but only as a friend and adviser. He had admitted his relationships with women were disastrous, as had his marriage been. 'What're you doing here, anyway?'

'I'm meeting an artist for a drink then I'm going to her place to take a look at her work. I've heard it's good. Do you want to join us? She's new to the area, she might be in need of a female friend.'

'No, not today, Geoff. I've got too much to do. Thanks all the same.'

'Okay. I'll be in touch.'

Rose wandered around the narrow lanes for a while then made her way home. She had no idea what the possible good news might be but Geoff would never tell anyone anything until he was certain it would happen. And who was this new painter? So many artists moved to the area because of the unique light, but also because of its history of artists. The work of the Newlyn School, formed in the 1880s, was becoming even more popular since *The Seine Boat* painted by its founder, Stanhope Forbes, had sold at auction for over a million pounds the previous year.

Rose spent the rest of the afternoon in the attic sorting through her photography file and thinking about her next piece of work.

Sitting at the kitchen table the following morning, a coffee at hand, she amended her shopping list. Satisfied, she was about to drive out to one of the supermarkets on the edge of Penzance when the front doorbell rang. Even the postman used the side door so this had to be a stranger.

Having given up expecting a phone call she was astonished to see Miranda nervously peering up at her from the lower step. 'Mrs Trevelyan, I'm sorry to turn up unannounced but could you spare me a few minutes?'

'Of course I can. Come in. I'm in the kitchen. Coffee?'

'Yes, please.'

'Have a seat.' Miranda was hovering in the doorway and seemed to be regretting her impulse to come. There was still plenty of coffee in the filter jug, all Rose had to do was to pour it. 'Is this about Joel?' she asked when they were both seated, milk and sugar on the table.

'Yes. In a way.'

'Now you're back can't you telephone him, or go and see Petra?' Miranda was in Newlyn, there was nothing to stop her calling on her relatives who lived only a mile and a half away.

'I'm too embarrassed to. Oh, it's all such a mess and I can't talk to Mum, even less so to Wendy.'

'Miranda, I don't know why you've come to me, other than I can see you have a need to talk. Look, would it be easier for you if I told you what I know about your family and then we can take it from there?'

'Yes, that's a good idea.' She picked up her mug and sipped the hot coffee which she drank black and sugarless like Rose. She watched her hostess as she listened. There was something soothing and calm about her, something which made it seem as if everything would turn out all right. As on the first occasion she had met her, Rose was dressed in

123

the colours of autumn; her hair, a shade lighter than copper beech, accentuated the effect. She was very attractive but in a more natural way than her mother, Louisa.

Rose summed up her knowledge briefly. 'Your father disappeared just at the time you were all moving. As did you, giving up your university place. Your aunt moved in with your mother and all contact was broken with the Penhaligons even though your uncle was so concerned about you he contacted the police.'

'Did he?' Miranda was genuinely surprised. Her brown eyes widened and colour came into her face. 'You know more than I do, in that case. What trouble I've caused.'

Rose assessed her. 'No, I don't think that's the case, I think you must've had good reason to do what you did. Did your mother know where you were?'

'No. I left a note saying I wasn't ready for university, that I didn't want to live on Bodmin Moor and I thought the time was right for me to start a new life.'

'No other explanation?'

'I didn't think she needed one.'

'Wasn't that a bit cruel? Roger told me you were close to her.'

'Not under the circumstances.'

And what circumstances were those? Rose wondered. Did the girl know what had happened to her father and want no part in it?

'I was afraid.' Miranda spoke without prompting. Her head was bowed, her face hidden beneath her hair.

'Afraid of what?'

'Of too many questions being asked. I don't know what

124

Dad did, only that there was some sort of scandal which was hushed up. No one would discuss it with me. Oh, don't get me wrong, I knew what he was like as a man, everyone did. He was greedy and there were other women. Aunt Wendy said no female was safe from him but she tends to exaggerate where Dad is concerned. I don't think she's ever liked him, not good enough for her sister, that sort of thing. And I'm pretty sure he was in debt. No, I know he was.'

'What did he do for a living?'

Miranda stared at Rose, unsure why she had used the past tense. 'He was a financial adviser, but he always seemed to have more money than the business could have provided. Joel once told me he owed money to Uncle Roger.'

Rose nodded. Here was another reason for someone wanting him out of the way. Or was it? A dead man could not repay his debts. But maybe he'd borrowed from the wrong sort of people. Don't be fanciful, she told herself, echoing Barry's words. 'Have you any idea where your father went?'

'None whatsoever.'

The answer was positive enough but the slight hesitation before it was given told Rose she was hiding something, if not lying. 'Why are you really here, Miranda? What is it you want from me?'

'I want to see Joel, I thought you might be able to help me.'

'You want me to act as an intermediary?'

'Yes.'

'In that case I'll need to know more. You see, I can't think of any reason why you can't contact your own family yourself.'

125

'As I said, they'll ask too many questions.'

Rose was becoming exasperated. 'About what?'

'About my father and where I've been.'

'The latter no longer seems to be a secret and the former, if what you've said is true, isn't a problem either. If you don't know where he went or why, you can't tell them, can you?'

'I don't *know* where he went, but I've got a good idea.'

'Miranda—'

She was on her feet so swiftly that she almost knocked over her chair. 'I'm sorry, I shouldn't have come.'

'Wait a minute. Sit down. Why don't you tell me what's really bothering you?'

'I can't. I really can't. Besides, you'd never believe me.'

'Did you know that there was a piece in the paper about your father? A firm of solicitors are trying to trace him.'

'Oh, God.'

'Do you think they'll find him, Miranda?' She could hardly ask if she thought he'd been murdered.

'I don't know. Mrs Trevelyan, there's one other thing. Why did my mother and aunt want their portraits painted?'

'They didn't say.'

Miranda nodded. 'There're all those other paintings, too, you must've seen them. If my father disappeared because he was in debt, how can they exist? Why didn't he sell them?'

'Perhaps they weren't his to sell.'

'But my mother—' She stopped abruptly

'Another coffee?'

'No thanks. I really must be going. They'll be wondering where I am. I told them I was going for a drive.'

126

So much deceit, Rose thought as she watched the girl walk down the drive towards the car which was parked in a lay-by on the opposite side of the road. 'Miranda,' she called. 'Do you still want me to speak to Joel?'

Her hair flew about her shoulders as she spun around. 'Would you?' she asked, smiling broadly. 'Ask him if he'll meet me tomorrow during his lunchtime. In our usual place. He'll know.'

'How can I get back to you?'

'There's no need. I'll be there anyway. If he doesn't turn up then I'll know he doesn't want to see me.' Miranda waved and then she was gone.

Rose had a lot to think about as she made her way along the seafront and out towards the supermarket. Here was a peculiar family with a lot to hide from one another. But now she was convinced that Louisa and Wendy had a reason to want Frank Jordan out of the way. Surely Miranda had hinted as much.

Joel said very little when Rose passed on Miranda's message after the class that evening. As far as he knew, his father had not acted upon Rose's information, had made no attempt to contact his niece. But listening to the students' many good wishes for Christmas and the New Year, Rose watched Joel and saw how pleased he was. 'Will you tell your parents about Miranda wanting to see you?'

'Not if she doesn't want me to.'

More secrets, Rose thought. Ought I to tell Jack that the girl's safe? No, he had admitted there was no case, that his hands were tied, and Roger, who had been worried, knew that his niece was back. That was the main thing. And Jack would accuse her of meddling, which of course she was by passing on Miranda's message.

Having secured the building she turned the corner and walked down Chapel Street, past the Egyptian House and the Union Hotel where the death of Nelson had first been announced. Here were small shops, individual in design and the goods they sold, but all of historical interest. She was meeting Barry in the Admiral Benbow, a pub and restaurant which boasted an ancient smugglers' tunnel which ran down to the sea. From there they were going for a curry. It would make a change from the seasonal menus most places were advertising.

The evening was balmy with a hint of a sea fret. Any frosts would come after Christmas, if they came at all. Rose was warm in her padded jacket. She unbuttoned it and tucked her hair behind her ears.

Barry was standing at the bar with two glasses in front of him. After so many years he knew Rose's preferences. Red wine tonight, which she always drank with a curry; she would not wish to mix her drinks beforehand.

'Just the one, then we'll eat or it'll be a bit of a rush,' Barry said.

In the short time they were in the upstairs bar the sea fret had thickened. Droplets of moisture hung in the air beneath the occasional lamp affixed to the buildings and muffled their footsteps as they crossed the road. There were no streetlights to illuminate the partially cobbled winding street.

'So you're match-making now,' Barry commented when Rose described Miranda's visit and Joel's reaction that evening.

'No.' Rose studied the menu. 'They're very fond of each other, but not in that way.'

'What if her mother or his father finds out?'

'I haven't done anything illegal Barry.'

'No, but the girl could easily have picked up the phone. Why all the secrecy? And why are you in collusion with them?'

'Whose side are you on?'

'Yours, Rose. Always yours, you know that. But you may have overstepped the mark this time.'

'God, you men are all the same. I'm only trying to help.'

Barry thumbed his glasses into place. 'No, you're not. You want to find out what's going on. Maybe we should pick up a couple of shovels and see if we can dig up the body.'

'Don't be facetious.'

The waiter approached their table and they gave their order. 'Have you heard from Jack?' Barry asked, hoping he had managed to sound conversational.

'Yes. He's coming on Christmas Eve and he's bringing Anna.'

'Oh?' Barry's grin was wry.

Rose blushed. He had guessed her motives for the invitation. 'There are no hard feelings. I couldn't not ask him. You're still going to act as my host, I hope.'

'Naturally.'

'Good.'

The meal arrived and they ate their baltis in silence for a few minutes. Tomorrow Joel would be reunited with his cousin. Rose would have loved to be present. Unfortunately there would be no opportunity to speak to him until after the break when classes resumed, unless he contacted her, or Miranda did.

'This Frank Jordan, have you heard any more?' Barry might have been reading her mind.

'No.'

'Then maybe he's turned up, collected his inheritance or whatever, and gone back to wherever he came from.' It was a possibility but seemed unlikely.

'What do you think they did with the body. Rose? What would you have done?'

'Oh, drop it, you'll give me indigestion.'

'I'm serious. Come on, give me your views.'

She put down her fork and leant forward, her forearms resting on the table. 'All right, here's what I think happened.'

As she explained, Barry's jaw dropped. 'You'd have made as good a criminal as an artist,' he said when she had finished. 'Bloody ingenious if you're right.'

Rose sipped her wine, pleased that Barry hadn't laughed at her. And how it would teach Jack Pearce a lesson if indeed she was right.

Dressed in jeans, sweatshirt and a short woollen jacket Miranda felt more like her old self as she waited for Joel. As children, the churchyard with its crumbling tombstones had fascinated them. They used to make up stories about the people who occupied the ancient vaults. Now, on a grey December day with a fine drizzle dampening her clothes, the place seemed very ordinary to Miranda.

They saw each other simultaneously Miranda jumped

up from the marble surround of the grave upon which she had been sitting and walked towards Joel. How quickly all those months fell away. It was as if she had never left. And how little I've thought of Michael since my return, she realised. She had spoken to him twice but there had seemed little to say. Maybe she had seen him as her salvation in London but no longer needed him now that she was home.

'How are you?' Joel asked quietly, noticing the change in Miranda. Once he would have hugged her without thinking, now he held back. She seemed more mature and fashionable although she was thinner and her face was pinched. Beside her he felt ridiculous in his sixth form uniform which served to accentuate the difference in their ages.

'I'm fine. You?'

Joel shrugged. 'Okay. Why didn't you write?'

They both sat on the edge of the grave, their hands in their pockets. Moisture clung to their hair and their clothes but neither of them noticed. 'I don't know. There were things going on that I didn't understand and no one would talk to me about them.'

'You could've talked to me.'

'I didn't want to involve you.'

'We were all worried sick.'

'I know that now. Maybe what I did seems wrong, but I meant it for the best.'

'You know about your father, I take it?'

'What about him?' There was a hint of panic in her voice.

'Take it easy. I only meant someone wants to find him.'

'Oh, that.' She sighed and when she looked up there were tears in her eyes. 'I missed you all so much, Joel. You mightn't believe me, but it's true.'

'We missed you, too. Do you want to tell me about it, about the real reason you disappeared like that?'

She nodded. 'But this is between ourselves. You must swear to me that it goes no further.'

'I give you my word.'

But when she had finished talking Joel doubted if he would be able to keep to that promise for ever.

CHAPTER TEN

'An' Cyril, he says to me, he says, "Make sure you take Rose some of my carrots. She can do some of they flower-shaped garnishes like they do in fancy restaurants." Not that Cyril would know, bless 'un, but he do like to look at them cookery programmes because of the veg.'

Laura, head tilted, winked at Rose. Doreen Clarke, a stiff white apron secured around her sturdy body, was in her element and had not stopped talking since her arrival an hour earlier. She liked both Rose and Laura and to be spending Sunday morning in Rose's kitchen helping to prepare the food for the Christmas Eve buffet was a pleasure she would not have missed. All that they were preparing that day could be frozen. Rose and Laura were concentrating on flans and pastry, Doreen's contribution would be two large gateaux. She was a self-taught cook. Having learnt basic skills from her mother she had finally surpassed her in talent.

'Course, I said to Cyril 'tweren't no good bringing 'un over yet. They've got to be fresh and cut up on the day. But don't you worry none, I'll see to them myself and bring them over on the night. I'll drop 'un in a bowl of iced water and they'll keep lovely.'

Rose shook her head imperceptibly, keeping her eyes on the mixer in which the pastry dough was turning. If she even glanced at Laura they would both start laughing.

There was barely room for the three of them to work but they'd organised themselves well; Rose one side of the kitchen, Laura on the other where she was slicing steak and vegetables for the pasties. Doreen, at the table in the middle of the room, was surrounded by various icing nozzles and food colourings. She had insisted upon mixing everything by hand. The sponges were already in the oven and could be smelt as they cooked.

'Your man at sea, then?' she asked Laura, unable to bear a lull in the conversation.

'Yes. He's landing on Tuesday. This is his last trip until the New Year.'

'You'll be pleased to see 'en, then, maid. It's always a worry when they're out there.' Doreen no longer considered the danger Cyril had been in when he had worked down the mine. Those days were long over and she had forgotten what it was like to wait for the siren to herald the change of shift when he would rise to the surface and safety. That was in the days before they had moved to Hayle.

'I think we deserve a break,' Rose said, wiping her hands on the dishcloth. On the worktop were pastry circles cut from around the edge of a saucer. Full-size pasties were out of the question as there was other food. All that would be left to do on the day was to mix the salads and lay out the bread, cold meats and cheeses.

Rose filled the kettle to make coffee as the filter machine had been moved to make room for the baking. Doreen and Laura cleared a space at one end of the table and sat down. 'I've bought a new frock, specially,' Doreen announced, her smile immediately changing to a frown.

Rose, with her back to the kitchen door, turned to see what had caught her attention. Beyond the glass panes Wendy Penhaligon had raised her hand, about to knock.

Rose opened the door. Wendy's face was grim. Maybe the sisters now regretted paying her account in full and she had come to ask for a refund.

'I'm sorry. I should've telephoned. I didn't realise you'd have company.'

'It doesn't matter. Come in, we're about to have coffee.' Odd, Rose thought, having driven a fair distance both Wendy and Miranda had arrived on the off-chance she would be at home and alone.

'Not for me, thank you. I can't stop.' She remained in the doorway, her pose rigid. Beneath a winter coat she wore a smart suit and blouse, a costume she might have worn to church. This was likely as congregations were larger in Cornwall than in many other places and Methodism was still strong.

'I just came to ask a favour.' She glanced at the two women seated at the table. 'I'd like you to leave my family alone. You had no business arranging a meeting between my nephew and niece.'

Doreen and Laura were gaping at the unknown woman. When Rose spoke they turned to look at her. 'Miranda is an

135

adult and quite capable of making her own decisions. She wanted to see Joel, I simply passed on a message. I did not arrange a meeting and I don't know if they even met.'

'They did. It has upset Miranda tremendously and it has upset her mother even more.'

It's upset you, Rose thought, not the others. And why not telephone? Because Wendy Penhaligon wanted to say more than she felt free to do in front of strangers. 'I meant no harm, and I cannot believe any has been done. Two cousins who are fond of each other have been reunited, that's all.'

'That isn't all, Mrs Trevelyan, not by a long way. You have no idea what trouble this has caused us all.' Her face reddened as she took a step forward. 'You can't possibly understand.'

Rose understood one thing: the sisters certainly had something to hide. 'May I ask you something? Was Miranda's homecoming the reason you changed your minds about the portrait? You see, it was purely by chance that I discovered your relationship with Joel and his family, there was nothing more sinister than that. He attends my classes and I had to speak to his parents on one occasion. I believed we were getting on quite well, you asked me to come to you, yet now I'm made to feel as if I was an intruder, as if I've done something wrong by meeting you in the first place.

'I didn't invite you here and you could quite easily have telephoned. Neither did I invite Miranda, she, too, came of her own accord. My class has now broken up until the New Year so I have no reason to see Joel until then. Miss Penhaligon, whatever your family secrets, they are

136

no concern of mine. I merely wanted to help an unhappy young woman.' She, too, had reverted to a more formal mode of address.

Rose did not see it coming. The colour drained from Wendy's face. White with rage she took another step forward and struck Rose on the side of the face.

'Well I never,' Doreen said, her hand to her mouth in shock.

Laura remained motionless. Rose had been in scrapes before but she had no idea what this one involved or why it had provoked such a violent reaction.

Wendy gasped, ashamed of her outburst. 'I apologise, Rose. I don't know what came over me, I don't usually lose my temper. I'll go now, but I would be grateful if you'd respect our privacy in future.' Whatever happened she did not want Louisa to be reunited with the rest of the family.

Rose watched her leave, one hand to her cheek which was stinging. Wendy had a violent streak, one which, despite what she had said, required little to arouse it.

'Good job they've already paid your bill,' Laura commented philosophically, allowing Rose a few seconds in which to compose herself. 'I thought perhaps she'd changed her mind and come to ask for a refund.'

'So did I.'

'That must be Louisa's sister, if I'm not mistaken. And her reckoning on being a lady. Just wait till I tell my Cyril.'

'Let's have another coffee,' Laura said, getting to her feet. 'And a fag. I need one even if you don't,' she added to Rose. 'And then you'd better tell your Aunty Laura what you've got yourself involved in now.'

137

'It's about Frank Jordan, that's what it's about, you mark my words,' Doreen interrupted. 'They were advertising for 'un in the paper and her, that Wendy, always had her eye on him, or so I've heard. Course, he married the younger, better-looking sister, and who can blame 'un. Not that it did Louisa much good in the end, she was never enough for that man. It wouldn't surprise me if Wendy knew where Frank was as we speak.'

Laura looked from one to the other. She still had no idea what her friends were talking about.

Rose accepted the coffee gratefully then explained the whole situation, apart from her suspicions concerning Frank's disappearance, uncaring that Doreen would probably repeat the tale to anyone who was prepared to listen.

'Does Jack know?' Laura saw no reason not to bring up his name.

'Yes, but there's nothing he can do. You know what I'm like, always imagining there's more to something than there really is.'

'But mostly you're right. What do you think's happened to Frank?'

Rose shook her head. She would discuss it with Laura later when Doreen had gone. To suggest someone had killed him, which had now crossed her mind, one of his family at that, would leave her open to a charge of slander if any of them ever found out. 'He's probably gone off with another woman and hasn't seen the advert.'

'Yes, well, men like that always come to a bad end. It's the law of nature, my girl, you mark my words.'

It was Laura who left first as she was expecting a phone call from one of her sons. Doreen followed soon after. 'Put some witch hazel on that cheek,' she advised as she pulled on her teacosy hat. ''Twill stop any bruising.'

Rose took the last of the flans out of the oven and set it to cool. She thought over what Doreen had said about Wendy's feelings for Frank. Miranda claimed Wendy had disliked her father, which may have been an act to disguise what she really felt, or it may have been genuine dislike caused by resentment and jealousy, a woman spurned. It must have been painful for Wendy, seeing the man she wanted married to another woman, and that woman her sister which meant they would come into regular contact. Was that reason enough for wishing him dead?

'Stop it,' she muttered as she turned off the oven. 'Why do you persist in thinking he's dead?'

She needed to clear her head. It was some time since anyone had attacked her physically and she was more shaken than she had allowed Doreen and Laura to see. She pulled on a coat, checked the sky for non-existent rain clouds and walked down the hill and turned right towards Penzance. Halfway along the Promenade she began to feel better. Fresh air and exercise always had that effect. Later she would have a bath, make something to eat and maybe watch some television instead of reading. For ten minutes or more she leant on the railings and watched the turnstones at work as they scrabbled among the pebbles. They were so well camouflaged that they were only distinguishable at first by the sound of skittering stones as they pushed them over with their beaks to search for food. Once Rose spotted one she looked more closely and realised there must be almost twenty working their way systematically along the beach.

The sky remained blue and the sea was now aquamarine with purplish patches where it covered Larrigan rocks. Black-headed gulls, now with their winter plumage of twin spots of black on each side of their heads, competed with the frill of water on the shoreline for whiteness. As it lapped against the granite slabs at the edge of the sand, the sun shot rainbow colours through the droplets of spray.

A dog raced along the beach, barking madly. It flushed the turnstones who flew off as one, their white undersides now visible, their thin cries clearly heard. Rose decided it was time to go home.

There was one message on the answering-machine. Roger Penhaligon asked her to ring back. Rose sighed. After her encounter with his sister that morning she felt disinclined to do so. It might be that he, too, was furious. Coward, she thought, as she picked up the phone. It was nearly three on a bright Sunday afternoon. The chances were he would be out and she, in turn, could also leave a message.

Petra Penhaligon answered on the fourth ring. 'I'm pleased you called, Rose.' There was friendship, not animosity in her voice. 'We're having a bit of a drinks party on Wednesday and we'd very much like you to come. I know it's short notice but we only decided this morning. We're off to Madeira for Christmas but Roger said we ought to at least invite a few people around before we leave.'

Wednesday. But her classes had finished. 'Thank you, I'd love to come. Shall I bring a bottle?'

'Certainly not. Just yourself and a guest if you like. Come any time after six-thirty.'

There had been no reference to Miranda or Joel. Presumably their meeting was still a secret in that household. If Joel hadn't mentioned it, why had Miranda?

Rose's hand was still on the receiver. She would make two calls then have that bath. In an hour or so it would be dark. The sun was already lower in the sky and the blueness had faded to the colour of pearls.

'We'll go by cab,' Barry Rowe said when she invited him to accompany her to the Penhaligons'.

'You order one from Stone's and pick me up. I'll pay for it.'

Her second call was more difficult. Rose had lost track of Jack's working pattern but decided to try him at home first. If he was there with Anna he might resent the interruption. She would not allow herself to think of what she might be interrupting. He'd almost certainly refuse her request anyway. Jack was at home but whether or not Anna was with him Rose didn't find out.

She began by telling him about Roger's party and although she had had no intention of mentioning his sister's behaviour she found herself talking about it quite naturally, just as she would have done in the days before Anna.

'Do you want me to arrest her for ABH?' He was only partly joking.

'Of course not. But doesn't it prove there's something going on? What difference does it make otherwise if Miranda and Joel see each other?'

'Oh, there's something going on, all right, Rose. You've

141

stepped in again where you've no business to be. Now, why did you really ring me?'

He's seen through me again, she thought, not allowing his penultimate remark to anger her. 'I know you'll say no, but I wanted to ask you a favour.'

'Go on. Ask away.'

'Well, I don't suppose there's any chance of you contacting that firm of solicitors to see if Frank Jordan has been in touch.' It was more of a statement than a question.

'Already done, my flower.' After Penhaligon's telephone call and what he had learnt from Rose, Jack had felt obliged to at least make some simple inquiries.

'What?' And you didn't tell me, you sod, she thought, wondering just how far they had drifted apart. More reasonably she saw that, as a policeman, there was no reason at all for him to have told her.

'No news yet so they're advertising nationally.'

'I see.'

'You're determined to make a mystery out of this, aren't you? How many people do you know who bother to read the personal columns?'

'I just thought . . .'

'That you know best. No mystery about it, he's left his wife and moved away. He's probably helping his new woman wash up the Sunday lunch dishes as we speak.'

Rose ignored the sarcasm. There were several occasions when she had been proved right and Jack knew that. 'Did they say why they wanted him to contact them?'

'Usual thing. As you guessed, a legacy. The last of his elderly aunts died recently.'

'Does Louisa Jordan have any claim to part of it?'

'How do you mean?'

'Well, as far as I'm aware they're not divorced. He buggered off on the day they were due to move and she's not heard a word from him since.'

'So she tells you. It may not be true. And your language hasn't improved with age.'

'Oh, dear. My apologies. I didn't mean to ruffle the nice policeman's sensibilities.'

'It's never stopped you before. Now, if that's all, I've got a few things to do, I'll speak to you soon.'

'Bye, Jack.' Rose did not ask what those things might be. She remained by the telephone table chewing a thumbnail while she digested what Jack had told her. It all sounded plausible and Louisa's husband would be the right age to have an elderly aunt. Rose shook her head. Plausible, yes, but Jack had not met the family and therefore was unable to sense the undercurrents which ran through it.

Forget it, she told herself as she went upstairs to run the bath.

Miranda, her mother and her aunt were walking on Bodmin Moor. All three were wrapped up against the cold wind which blew across the flat landscape despite the brightness of the day. Miranda had been home for almost three weeks and was finally beginning to loosen up. She still wasn't sure why she had admitted to seeing Joel. There had been too many secrets in the past and she wanted some honesty now. Perhaps she had hoped to draw her mother out. She had talked about her flat and job and now, as they walked, she spoke of how she had met Michael.

'How do you feel about him?' Louisa asked.

'I'm not certain. I thought I was sure when I was in London but everything seems different now that I'm back.'

Louisa took her arm. Any chance to be tactile was welcome. 'And now? Today?'

'I miss him. I suppose there's been too much else to think about for me to analyse it properly.'

'If you're not sure then he isn't for you.' Wendy spoke with conviction. It was one of her few remarks since they had left the house. She had been mostly silent since her return from Newlyn knowing she ought never to have acted as she had done. In fact, going there at all had been a big mistake. It was always better to leave things be.

'Mum, could I ask him to come down? That way, seeing him out of his own surroundings, I might get a clearer picture of my feelings. It isn't fair for me to keep him hanging on if it isn't going to work.'

'What a good idea. Why not ask him for Christmas if he has no plans? What do you say to that, Wendy?'

Wendy kept her eyes on the ground. 'Our household grows larger by the minute. But it's entirely your decision, Louisa – it is, after all, your house.'

Mother and daughter exchanged a look of surprise. There was bitterness in those words and Wendy had been acting strangely ever since Miranda's return. 'But you share it, and you pay your way. I wouldn't want you to feel uncomfortable.'

'I know. I'm sorry. I think, maybe, I'm coming down with something. I'm not myself at all at the moment. Of course he must come.' Her sister must never be allowed to know that she was jealous of Miranda. For the first time in her life Wendy had had Louisa to herself.

'Then phone him tonight, Miranda,' Louisa said. The matter settled, they retraced their steps and went back to the house for the Sunday roast which they had decided to eat in the early evening.

The dishes washed and put away, Miranda rang Michael who was thrilled to be invited. 'My parents won't mind. In fact, they'll probably be relieved. My sister and her husband will be there and they've just had a baby. He's the centre of attention at the moment.' He made a note of the directions Miranda gave him. 'I'll see you next week. I can't wait, I've really missed you,' he said before he hung up.

Wendy, who had been listening to half of the exchange, said she was having an early night. 'I really feel under the weather, I do hope I'm not ill for Christmas.'

'Do you fancy a drink?' Louisa asked when Wendy had gone. It was the first time she had been properly alone with her daughter. 'We've got almost everything.'

'I'd love one.'

They sat in armchairs each side of the blazing fire, their legs stretched out, their drinks in their hands. Until that moment neither of them had realised the strain that Wendy's constant attendance had produced.

'Can you tell me, darling, why you left the way you did?' Louisa finally asked what had been on her mind since she had first seen Miranda on the doorstep.

'No, Mum. Please don't ask me. It just seemed the right thing to do at the time.'

'To leave without saying goodbye, to not tell me you were safe and well? I've been worried sick and I missed you so badly. I know you left a note but it wasn't enough, Miranda. I feel you owe me some sort of explanation. Were you with your father? I know things weren't always good between the two of you but I thought you might've gone with him.'

Miranda met her mother's eyes and knew that she had been extremely stupid. She had got things very wrong. 'No. I wasn't with him. I told you I had my own flat in London. I've no idea where he is.'

'Then why? You'd have been at university, you needn't have come here if you didn't want to, in the vacations, I mean. You gave up so much. Tell me, was any of it to do with Wendy? She's been acting very oddly since you came back.'

'No. It isn't.' Miranda felt the heat in her face, it was a lie, but a necessary one because her view of what had taken place the previous year had altered radically.

'Then why are you and she so distant? She loved you almost as much as I did before we moved.'

'Maybe she's as disappointed in me as you are.'

'I'm not disappointed in you, I don't care what you do with your life as long as you're happy and healthy.'

Tears filled Miranda's eyes. She should have stayed and faced things out, she had been mistaken about her mother, maybe all the rest of it was also a mistake. 'Do you have any idea what happened to Dad?'

Louisa shook her head. 'None whatsoever. One minute he was there, packing his things, the next he had gone. He only took one suitcase and his personal papers. He must've planned it months in advance.

'As I said, things hadn't been good, he had financial problems, but he seemed as keen as I was on the move. I thought it would provide us with a second chance, just the two of us, away from everything we knew, away from temptation . . . Obviously I was a fool to imagine it would work out.'

'You still loved him despite . . .'

'Despite the other women.' She smiled wryly. 'Oh, I knew about them but there weren't as many as rumour would have it. They were affairs, nothing serious, I always thought he'd stay with me.'

'But how do you cope, financially? You're not divorced, I take it.'

'No, we're not. Your father sold the Penzance place and bought this one which was much less expensive, putting it in my name. I rather suspect the profit was used to pay off his overdraft because I haven't heard a word from the bank. He could never resist a business gamble. Sometimes they paid off, sometimes they didn't. Over the last few years he was becoming more reckless and consequently, more careless. I've no idea of the true state of his finances, all I know is that they haven't affected me. I've an income of my own, Wendy pays her share and the house is fully paid for.'

'Do you think he was using you?'

'In what way?'

'Well, once the house sale went through and he was solvent again perhaps he felt his conscience was clear. You were provided for so he could take off.' She prayed this was the case.

'Maybe.' Louisa threw a dry log on to the fire, unable to meet her daughter's eyes. Sparks flew up the chimney and the flames cast shadows around the room. Outside the wind was gaining strength. It howled eerily across the open moorland and whistled down the chimney, making them both wonder if there was any truth in the supposed sightings of wildcats in the area which might have been released from captivity when stricter laws regarding keeping such animals as pets had come into being.

Wishing to prolong this new intimacy with her daughter, Louisa suggested another drink.

'Didn't you have any idea he was going?' Miranda asked as she accepted the glass.

'No. Any more than I did about you.'

'I'm sorry, Mum. Can you ever forgive me?'

'I forgave you the moment I saw you.' She shook her head. 'Whatever your reasons at least you came home. I thought your father was still helping with the packing. I was down at the bank sorting out all those last minute things and when I got back he had gone. Wendy told me he simply picked up a suitcase and told her he was never coming back. She tried to stop him, to talk some sense into him, but he wasn't having it.' She shrugged as she studied her fingernails. 'I suppose one could say that it was typical of Frank. Anyway, that's in the past. I'm sure he'll get in touch if he ever wants a divorce.'

'Then it means he's still got some claim on this house.'

'Yes, I suppose it does. The law works both ways these

days. No doubt he can prove it was his money that bought it.'

'The day he left, Wendy told you all about that? Then she must've been alone in the house with him.'

'Yes. Why?' Louisa frowned, she was certain something was wrong between aunt and niece.

'Oh, nothing.' She paused. 'It was great seeing Joel again. I've been such a fool, not keeping in touch with anyone. I must've had a brainstorm, perhaps it was the thought of leaving everything I had ever known and loved.'

'What did you talk about, you and Joel?'

'Old times, what we'd both been doing. He's going to be an artist. Rose Trevelyan thinks he's got it in him. I liked her, Mum, I had a feeling she'd help me, just as Joel said she'd helped him.' If her mother knew what she had told Joel she would be horrified.

'But if you were so keen to see him why didn't you go to the house?'

'I was embarrassed. I wasn't sure what Uncle Roger and Petra would think of me after all this time, especially as they were so good to me. I just wouldn't have been able to explain why I hadn't kept in touch but I knew Joel would understand.'

But you haven't really explained your reasons to me, either, my darling, Louisa thought, but she knew better than to press Miranda that night. Her flimsy excuses didn't ring true but at least she had begun to talk. Wendy and Miranda suspect something, she thought, but I really can't imagine what. Not the truth, certainly they couldn't have picked on the truth.

'I'm tired, Mum, I think I'll go up. It must be all this

fresh air and exercise. It's a different kind of tiredness to what you feel in London, nicer, as if you've earned it somehow.' She leant over and kissed Louisa's cheek. 'See you in the morning.'

'Take a lamp.'

Miranda smiled. 'I keep forgetting. It's rather fun in a way.' She lit one and left the room.

The stairs creaked beneath her feet even though she weighed little. Passing Wendy's room she heard the light snores of someone starting a head cold. How can she sleep so soundly? Miranda wondered. How can she sleep at all? Yet I manage to sometimes, she realised as she placed the lamp on the bedside table.

Her shadow danced across the walls as she undressed. Five minutes later she was sleeping soundly.

Louisa leant back in her chair. Would she have to alter her plans? Would Miranda ever understand? And what about Wendy? What a fool she had been allowing her to move in. But I was lonely and missing Frank dreadfully, she admitted. As I still do.

She got up. It was time to go to bed.

CHAPTER ELEVEN

Barry Rowe was waiting on the pavement outside his shop when the taxi pulled up. The lane at the rear of the building was too narrow for traffic although he could reach his first-floor flat from there by way of a metal staircase. It could also be reached via stairs at the rear of the shop. 'Wow, very glam,' he said as he slid into the back seat beside Rose. Beneath her open coat was a silky dress in apple green. She had left her hair to fall loose around her shoulders and had spent more time than usual on her make-up.

'You don't look too bad yourself.' She glanced at his jacket. It was another new one. He had finally decided to spend some money on himself. And not before time, Rose thought.

'Will I know anyone?'

'I've no idea. Apart from Roger and Petra it's doubtful if I will either. But you never know.' The community within West Penwith was tight-knit, there was more than a chance they would meet someone they knew or someone who was a friend of someone they knew.

As they left the outskirts of Penzance Rose gave the driver directions. When they reached the house it was once again ablaze with lights but this time there were several cars parked in the spacious drive. Barry paid their fare as he had promised. Rose shivered. It had been hot in the taxi but the wind was blowing now, seemingly from several directions as her coat swirled at the hem and her hair was lifted and tossed around her face. Bare trees and evergreen shrubs rattled as they made their way to the front door.

Roger Penhaligon let them in. 'We're glad you could make it, Rose.' He shook Barry's hand, managing to manipulate a whisky glass and a thick cigar in his left hand as the introductions were made. 'We're not a big crowd, just a few friends. As we're deserting them all for Christmas we felt we ought to do our bit first.'

Money, Barry thought as he assessed his surroundings quickly, and plenty of it. These were the Penhaligons, the people with whom Rose had become involved. How many times had he told her not to get involved? How many times had Jack done so? But money was a powerful thing, the root of many crimes. Maybe she was right to take an interest in this family.

When they entered the lounge Rose was surprised to see Joel talking to contemporaries of his parents. She had imagined he would have taken himself off somewhere with some of his own. He smiled when he saw her and came over to say hello.

'This is Barry Rowe.' Rose wondered if Joel would come to the wrong conclusion about their relationship, and if he did, why it mattered.

'Hi. I'm Joel Penhaligon.'

To Barry's surprise he held out a hand. His grip was firm. The boy was more mature than he had expected, and better-looking.

'Let's not monopolise our celebrity guest, I want to show her off,' Roger said as he took Rose's elbow and led her around the room, introducing her to the other guests. Barry followed them doggedly, hoping that he could have Rose to himself for at least a part of the evening.

Petra was in the kitchen surrounded by trays of food. Either she was an excellent hostess or they had hired caterers. 'Hello, Rose.' She frowned. 'Do you think there's enough to go round?'

Rose grinned. 'Masses. What do you think, Barry?' But when she turned he had disappeared.

'I always worry when we entertain. I know those people are all old friends, but—'

'Everything looks fine, Petra,' Rose interrupted just as Barry returned and placed a glass in her hand. Rose thanked him. 'I didn't expect Joel to be here.'

'Neither did we. Duty dictated, I think. He suddenly decided he didn't want to come to Madeira with us so I assume he felt obliged to do his bit this evening.'

'What's he going to do over Christmas?'

Petra shrugged and brushed back her hair. 'Who knows what boys that age will do? I thought Roger would be furious but ever since you came that night he and Joel seem to have come to some sort of an understanding. Joel's given his word that there won't be any wild parties. We have to trust him. After all, he'll be eighteen in

January. A man. It doesn't bear thinking about.

'Anyway, we know he's spending Christmas Day with a friend and his family. The rest is up to him.'

'He's more than welcome to come to me if he needs a square meal,' Rose said, ignoring the scowl on Barry's face. 'When did he change his mind?'

'Last week. He simply announced he no longer wanted to come. Still, at that age few boys want to go away with their parents.'

Miranda, Rose thought. Joel had changed his mind since their meeting. How much did he know? How much had Miranda confided in him? Enough to give up the chance of a holiday? She would have loved to have been able to overhear their conversation.

She and Barry circulated and made the requisite small talk but it was not a party either of them particularly enjoyed. Money seemed to be the main topic of conversation, money and boats. Rose loved the sea, but only when viewed from the land. She was not a good sailor.

'Roger, did you follow up on what I told you?' she asked some time later when he was alone at the drinks table.

'About Miranda? No. It's enough to know that she's safe. She knows where we are if she needs us. Joel took the news very calmly. I was surprised.'

So Roger had told Joel that Miranda was back before I passed on her message, Rose realised, which explained his lack of surprise.

Just before they left Rose found an opportunity to speak to him. 'Look, I know you'll be on your own over Christmas. You've got my number, just give me a ring if you want to. I'll be more than happy to cook you a meal.'

'Thank you. I'll do that. Actually, I was going to ring you anyway.'

'Oh?'

Joel shook his head. What he wanted to say would have to wait, he could not discuss what was on his mind with so many people around.

A loud knock on the door let Rose and Barry know that their taxi had arrived. Barry looked relieved. Socialising was not one of his strong points and when he engaged in it he preferred more intimate gatherings. At least Rose hadn't known anyone other than their hosts, a fact which surprised him. 'Room for another drink?' he asked as they pulled out into the main road.

Rose glanced at her watch. Eight forty; it wasn't late. They had decided in advance that two hours was the optimum time to stay. To leave too early or to linger after others had gone would have seemed impolite. 'No, not tonight, Barry. I'm a bit tired.' And although she refused to admit it, she was still upset about Jack. An early night would do her good.

In bed she realised she had missed an opportunity to learn anything new about Frank Jordan and his family. The Penhaligons would be out of circulation for a while now.

For the next two days Rose was able to work outside. She had decided to paint the Minnack and its dramatic setting. The open-air amphitheatre was carved out of the cliffside and had spectacular sea views. To one side, way down, was a sheltered beach of fine white sand edged with an aquamarine sea. Ahead was the Atlantic ocean. She had been to many productions at the Minnack, once or twice with Jack, but she would not let those memories interfere with her work.

On the first day, Thursday, she found a spot out of the breeze, hoping it wouldn't change direction. She pulled on her fingerless gloves and surveyed the scene, deciding upon the best aspect. The myriad colours of the sea would take some capturing but she was sure she could do it. After twenty minutes she began preparing the blank canvas.

It was just what she had needed. Four uninterrupted hours of fresh air and pure concentration. Four whole hours without thinking about Jack or the Penhaligon family. She would have stayed longer but the December days were short and already the light was changing, the colours were no longer vibrant. She watched a cormorant skim the surface of the water before disappearing around the jagged cliffside. Shadows lengthened, altering the vista further. Impossible to work any longer.

The good weather lasted and by Friday afternoon Rose began to hope that the painting would turn out to be as good as the Zennor one. Sitting beneath a blue sky in which a few curls of white cloud had appeared she watched the gulls drift in the air currents. It was hard to believe it was almost Christmas. And I still have things to do, she remembered.

She stood and stretched, feeling the wind in her face once she was no longer protected by the rocky outcrop. Home. Home and a nice quiet evening.

Rose was in the kitchen, a glass of wine in her hand. It was dark but the house was warm and cosy. She studied the mackerel in front of her, head on one side. Grilled, she decided, because it was easiest.

The telephone rang. Quickly topping up her glass in case it was Laura wanting a long chat, she went to answer it.

'Is your offer still on, Mrs Trevelyan?' Joel asked.

'Of course.' Rose had wondered if he was being polite at the party. What teenage male would want to share a meal with a solitary middle-aged woman? Over the past two days she had put his eager response down to a drop too much of his father's excellent wine. But she hoped he didn't intend coming that night; she liked plenty of time to prepare when she was entertaining.

'Mum and Dad left this morning. I think I'll enjoy being alone in the house. Is tomorrow too soon?'

'Tomorrow's fine. What time would you like to come?'

Instead of answering the question he asked one of his own. 'Would you think it rude of me if I asked if I could bring someone?'

'Not at all.' Miranda, Rose thought. It has to be. 'Your cousin?'

'Yes.'

'Does her mother know?' Rose did not want a repeat of the scene with Wendy Penhaligon.

'Yes. She had to know because Miranda will be staying with me overnight. We have things to discuss.'

I'll bet, Rose thought, longing to know what they were. But the telephone was not the best medium by which to conduct the conversation she wanted to have with him. Tomorrow would do. Yet she sensed the young couple needed someone in whom to confide and that questions might be unnecessary. 'Good. Then come for lunch. Is there anything either of you don't eat?'

'No. Nothing at all.'

'In that case I'll expect you any time after twelve.' It would mean no work tomorrow but a day off wouldn't hurt. And her curiosity had been aroused anew. It was at such times she missed Jack badly. She could have invited him to make up a foursome and he could have formed his own opinion about her guests. Except, she realised, they probably wouldn't confide in her if there was someone else present.

Rose went back to the kitchen and prodded the vegetables. They were just beginning to tenderise. Perfect timing. The petrol colours of the mackerel gleamed. She placed it, whole, under the grill. Within minutes its rich, oily aroma made her realise how hungry she was.

Sitting at the kitchen table, the radio playing quietly, she planned the lunch she would prepare tomorrow.

At eight she rang her parents to confirm the Christmas arrangements. She still had no idea what to buy them. They seemed to have everything they needed. But time was running out. Monday was the twenty-third and the day of their arrival, that was the only morning left in which to shop. Something would catch her eye, it usually did at the last minute.

She had decided to cook a traditional roast for Joel and Miranda. She never bothered to do so just for herself. By eleven o'clock on Saturday morning the meat was in the oven and the vegetables were prepared. Rose went outside to inspect the garden. Her father was sure to comment upon its winter untidiness. She weeded the border at the side and cut back the geraniums in their pots. There was already new growth shooting out from the joints.

A car turned into the drive and came to a stop behind

hers. Miranda pulled hard on the handbrake because of the steepness of the drive. They had arrived fifteen minutes early.

'It's nice to see you both again,' Rose said with a smile as they got out. 'Come on in and we'll have a drink. Just let me wash my hands.' She dumped the plastic bag of garden rubbish in the bin and scraped the soil from her hands beneath the kitchen tap. 'Now what would you like? I've got beer, wine, sherry or something stronger.'

'Wine for me, please,' Miranda said as she unwound her scarf and shook out her hair.

'I'll have a beer,' Joel replied, wondering how on earth they could tell this woman what they suspected. But someone ought to know. It was not fair to Miranda to have to keep such knowledge to herself for ever. He realised he hadn't been totally shocked when she told him her fears. The same thought had crossed his mind in the beginning.

'Lunch won't be ready until one. Let's go into the sitting room. I've lit the fire.'

Sunshine spilt in through the window where Miranda and Joel stood admiring the view.

'If only you knew how much I've missed all this,' Miranda said with a sweeping gesture of her hand. 'I don't know how I stuck it in London for so long. Well, I'm back now.' She smiled at Rose. 'And back in contact with Joel, thanks to you.'

All three sat, Joel and Miranda on the two-seater settee, Rose in an armchair near the fire. Lighting it had not been necessary, it was merely a welcoming gesture. The sitting room door stood open so it wasn't too hot. 'You told me you didn't feel you could meet Roger and Petra,'

Rose began, wanting to break the ice. She could sense their slight discomfort. 'Was there any reason other than your embarrassment after such a long time?'

Miranda sighed. 'Yes. I didn't want them asking me questions about Dad. Mrs Trevelyan, I really don't know what to do. I might've wasted a year of my life over something which has been driving me mad even though I don't have any proof. Joel knows, and I think he agrees with me. Would you mind if I told you what it is?'

'No. And I can assure you I'll do or say nothing to anyone unless you wish me to.'

'I don't see what anyone can do.' She sipped her wine and placed the glass on the small table beside her. 'I think my father is dead. Everyone assumes he went off with another woman, but I don't think he'd have left Mum. When I look back on it I think he loved us. But when time passed and neither he nor my mother made any effort to find me I became more and more convinced that something was dreadfully wrong. I just couldn't face going home or even making contact in case I was right. Anyway, from things I've learnt I realise now that my mother had nothing to do with it.'

'I don't understand.'

'Oh, God, it sounds so melodramatic and ridiculous. I knew Mum wanted a new start and, at first, I thought she – well, I thought she might have got so fed up with his womanising and money troubles that she killed him. I now know that isn't so. Anyway, since I've been back Aunt Wendy's been acting pretty strangely, as if she doesn't want me around, yet we used to get on well. I mean, is it possible Wendy killed him? You know

160

both sides of the family a bit, do you think it's likely? Joel told me that Uncle Roger contacted the police several times but they aren't able to do anything.'

Rose had been certain there was more to Miranda's disappearance than a change of heart about university, just as certain as her uncle had been. She had run to protect her mother. She wondered if Miranda was asking for help and, if so, what she could do about it. 'Why would Wendy wish him any harm?'

'She never liked him, she was always saying he wasn't good enough for Mum, that he sponged off her, which wasn't true, and they should never have got married.'

'But what could she possibly achieve by his death?'

'Well, she's in a very comfortable position living with Mum. Maybe she and Dad had an argument. Mum told me that she was at the bank and the solicitor's office for most of the morning he disappeared. There's only Wendy's word that he took off at the last minute.'

'Miranda, I happen to know that your father hasn't yet responded to the advertisement. Of course, that doesn't mean anything, it was only in the local paper. The firm of solicitors are now advertising nationally. His aunt died, apparently. Did you know her?'

'I met her a couple of times when I was small. She lived in the Midlands, we didn't visit often. I think she went into a home when her husband died. She must have been quite an age.'

Rose glanced at Joel who had remained silent. 'What do you think about all this?'

'I don't know. It does seem odd. Uncle Frank seemed

keen to move, but it could've been a front. He might have planned his disappearance months in advance.'

'But?'

He looked up and shook his head. 'But why would he want to disappear? As Miranda said, he had everything he wanted as far as we know.'

Rose took a sip of her own drink. Maybe they'd all got it wrong. When people disappeared for no apparent reason those left behind felt lost and required answers. They also believed they had known the person, that they could swear they hadn't left of their own accord. But no one could see into someone else's head. It happened. Happily married men and women with children, a home and money had reasons no one could guess at for wanting to make a fresh start. Frank Jordan had possibly been one of them, especially once he believed his daughter was going to university.

'There's one thing I don't understand. He loved the sea, his boat meant everything to him. Why would he want to live in the middle of Bodmin Moor?'

'His boat? What happened to it?' Cornwall might be a large county lengthwise but Bodmin was no more than ten or fifteen miles from the coast in either direction. He'd still have been able to use it. 'Did he sell it?'

It was Joel who answered. 'We don't know. Dad even went down to the boathouse. It was locked but you can see through a gap in the planks and it wasn't there.'

'What sort of boat?'

'A cabin cruiser.'

Perhaps it was his means of escape. 'Could it have reached the Continent?'

'Yes. France, easily. But what would he do there? He doesn't have any connections overseas as far as I know,' Miranda said.

'Let me think about this for a few minutes. I'll just put the vegetables on. Help yourselves to another drink if you want one.' Rose left the room, unable to determine what she believed. It seemed that Miranda and Joel were unaware of Wendy's infatuation with Frank. If she had harmed him her feelings were far more of a motive than anything else Rose had learnt so far. Maybe she had been unable to bear the thought of him moving away and trying to make a go of it with Louisa. When they had all lived in Penzance she had seen him every day. If Louisa had been out of the way for the morning she might have begged him not to go. If Frank Jordan had rebuffed her again, laughed at her, how would a woman like Wendy react? Rose had seen for herself the violence of which she was capable. Oh, Jack, if only you were here, she thought as she basted the potatoes and parsnips with juices from the meat.

When she returned to the sitting room she refilled her own glass and sat down again. 'This boathouse. Where is it?'

'It's not really one, it's a lock-up place Dad bought years ago. More of a garage really.'

'Was it sold with the house?'

Miranda shrugged. 'Not as far as I know. It wasn't attached to the house, it wasn't anywhere near it, in fact.'

'I don't suppose you've got a key?'

'No. Why?'

Good question, Rose thought. But maybe it would

163

hold some clue to the man. Maybe he had used it for other reasons as well as storage space for the boat. If it had been sold there was nothing they could do. 'It might be worth taking a look at it.'

'We can't just break in. Even if it still belongs to Uncle Frank it would be illegal.' Joel was horrified.

'Miranda's his daughter,' Rose pointed out. 'If he still owns it it would be all right. Look, if he took the boat and he's still in the country wouldn't he have to register it somewhere?'

'I'm not sure how it works, but I suppose there'd have to be some record of it.'

Rose nodded. Could she ask Jack to check? Would he even bother? It was worth a try. Their faces flushed from the drinks and the heat of the fire, they sat in silence, each with their own thoughts. Rose began to understand Miranda's behaviour. If she had believed her own mother to have been involved in a murder, one solution was to disappear in order to evade any questions if the police were alerted. An immature solution but the girl had been only eighteen at the time. From what both Miranda and Joel had said, Rose knew that the mother and daughter had been very close. And there was Wendy's changed attitude. Was there a sinister reason for this or did she simply resent Miranda reappearing and disturbing their comfortable lifestyle? 'I think it's time to eat,' Rose said, picking up her glass as she stood. Miranda had not topped up her drink, she'd be able to have a second glass of wine with the meal.

'This is delicious,' Joel said as he cut the last of his roast potatoes.

He had eaten more quickly than either of the women. It pleased Rose to see her cooking appreciated. 'There's plenty more if you've room.'

'He's always got room,' Miranda told her with a smile. 'I don't know where he puts it all.'

He's probably still growing, Rose thought but did not say because it would have embarrassed him to be thought of as a boy still.

She had made a fruit salad to follow, thinking they would be too full for anything heavier, and she had bought some clotted cream. Joel dolloped several spoonfuls on his dish.

When they had finished Miranda offered to wash up but Rose said she would see to the dishes later. Unused to eating her main meal in the middle of the day she felt in need of a walk and therefore suggested one. 'We could take a look at the boathouse,' she said diffidently, as if the idea had just occurred to her. 'In the same way as your father did,' she added for Joel's benefit. 'Take a peep through the gap.'

Miranda thought it was a good idea. 'I could do with some exercise, too. How about it, Joel?'

He nodded, realising he had been outvoted by the women. He'd rather leave things alone. But I did promise to help Miranda, he thought, and his parents were away, they'd never find out.

Together they walked down the hill and along the front towards Penzance where they cut up behind the tennis courts and the bowling green to rows of terraced granite properties. Here was a labyrinth of alleyways and quaint buildings. At the end of one such street stood a garage.

There was just room to manoeuvre a car and boat from the main road running at right angles to it.

As the three of them stood looking at the lock-up they attracted the attention of a man living in the house opposite. He came out and stood in the tiny patch of front garden. 'Can I help you?' he asked, wondering if this unlikely threesome was about to break in.

'Ah, yes, maybe you can,' Rose said, turning on the charm as she smiled at him. 'We'd heard this was up for sale but there doesn't seem to be a board.'

'It's the first I've heard of it. A bloke called Jordan owns it but he hasn't been around for ages. He was always down here at one time making a meal of getting that boat in and out. The boat's gone, too.'

'Maybe that's why I heard the garage was for sale. Did he take it somewhere else?' Rose asked innocently.

'Never saw him if he did.' He turned away realising he had let them know the only way he could be aware of this fact was by looking through the gap.

'Thanks, anyway,' Rose called to his retreating back.

'What now?' Miranda asked. 'I could break the lock, but the old boy'll be watching us and ring the police.'

Rose eyed the small padlock. 'We'll come back later. If we leave now and get an appropriate tool, if he does see us he'll think we've obtained a key from somewhere. What do you think?'

'No,' Joel said.

'I don't see why not. I mean, it seems Dad does still own it, there's no reason for me not to have a look inside.'

They walked back and waited until the light began to

fade. Rose found a set of screwdrivers with which they could hopefully remove the whole padlock unit and then replace it. None of them had noticed if the screws were rusty.

It was colder when they left the house. Miranda offered to drive. She parked the car in the next street away from the prying eyes of the man they had seen earlier. The pensioner's curtains were drawn now. If he was watching television he probably wouldn't hear them.

'You do it,' Miranda said, handing Joel the screwdrivers.

It took longer than they had anticipated as one of the screws had gone in crooked but at last the whole unit came away in Joel's hands. He pushed open the creaking wooden door and they stepped inside.

'Close it behind you,' Rose told Miranda. When she had done so Rose switched on her flashlight.

'Oh, my God.' Miranda ran to the back of the building and stood looking down at something.

'What is it?' Rose hurried to her side.

'It's Dad's holdall.'

'What? Are you certain?'

'Yes, I saw him pack it. We'd all decided to keep out the clothes we needed for the first couple of days. Look, there's his initials.'

Rose had no idea what to do. Jack ought to be informed immediately 'Can you bear to open it, Miranda?' It had been there some time, there were patches of mould on its surface.

She nodded but there were tears in her eyes. She bent down and unzipped the bag. The clothes were damp but instantly recognisable. 'His passport's here, too, and his driving licence. Oh, Rose, I was right, something awful's happened to him.'

Rose put her arms around her. 'Don't cry. This doesn't prove anything. But we need some help now, some official help. Are you prepared to talk to the police? There's someone I know who'll listen.' I hope, she added silently.

Miranda sniffed as she nodded. 'They'll have to listen this time.'

'You were right to insist we did this, Mrs Trevelyan,' Joel said. He looked worried and frightened.

'It'll mean dragging Mum into it, but we can't ignore this.' Miranda pointed to her father's possessions.

'Okay Joel, can you get that padlock back on. We need to make the place secure and I think we ought to leave the bag where we found it.'

Joel got to work. Rose and Miranda stood, shivering in the chilly evening air, until he had finished.

'Will you come back to my house?' Rose asked. 'It'll be easier if we're all together.'

They drove back, all grateful that the Penhaligons were on holiday and that Wendy and Louisa were in Bodmin. Maybe something useful could be achieved before any of those people learnt what they had done.

CHAPTER TWELVE

'Would you get that?' Jack called from the kitchen where he was cooking pasta for their supper.

'Okay.' Anna went to answer the phone. It was already dark outside. A streetlight cast its light on the roof of Jack's car. Absent-mindedly she gave the number. 'Yes, he's here. I'll get him,' she said before laying the receiver on the table.

'Jack, it's Mrs Trevelyan. She says it's important or she wouldn't have rung.' Jack stood in the kitchen doorway, a fork in his hand.

He crossed the hall and went into the lounge. Anna looked vaguely annoyed. 'I'll see to the rest of the meal,' she said, not wishing to hear his side of the conversation.

'What is it, Rose?' He listened for several minutes. 'You're right, it does seem important, although it could be he decided to ditch his clothes at the last minute.'

'And his passport and driving licence?'

'You have a point. Ring the station and tell them exactly what you've told me. I imagine someone will want to speak to you all tonight.' They'll certainly take a look at that bag, he thought.

'Can't you come yourself?'

'I'm off duty.'

'I meant as a friend.'

'Rose, I—'

'Sorry, Jack. I shouldn't have asked. I realise Anna's there with you.'

Jack felt a wave of regret. He wanted to go, he wanted to see Rose and he wanted to hear more about what they had discovered. But he could hardly ditch Anna. He had invited her over for the evening and their meal was almost ready.

'What did she want?' Anna asked when he returned to the kitchen.

'It's a long story. It involves a person who has disappeared. I won't bore you with it now. She wanted me to go over there but I advised her to ring Camborne.'

'I see.' Her face was serious.

'What do you see, Anna?' He tilted her chin up with his forefinger.

'Jack, this isn't going to work, is it?'

'What isn't?'

'Us.'

'Why shouldn't it? We hardly know each other yet. I enjoy your company, Anna, I like being with you very much.'

'The same goes for me, but – well, I just feel that sometimes a part of you is elsewhere.'

'It comes with the job. I did warn you there'll be late nights, times when I can't keep to an arrangement.'

'It isn't the job, Jack. It's her. Rose.'

'Rose is a thing of the past. Why won't you believe me?'

Anna ran a hand through her dark hair. 'Because I saw

your face when I said her name and I can tell that you really want to go to her. And you would've done if I wasn't here.'

Fair comment, Jack thought. I would have done. But you are here, Anna, and I didn't. Yet she had been astute enough to sense his feelings. 'I don't know what to say. The fact is I didn't go and our pasta will be overcooked.'

'I've drained it.'

'It'll be cold then,' he said with a smile, trying to lighten the mood. 'Come on, let's eat.'

She shook her head. Her face was pale and disappointment showed in her eyes. 'I'm not hungry now. I think I'll go home. Forgive me, I don't mean to sound like a petulant teenager but I've been in a similar position before and I'm not prepared to play second best. Rose may no longer want you but until you're certain you feel that way about her, too, it's better if we don't see each other.'

'Anna, please.' He took her arm and turned her to face him. So this was what had been on her mind. He knew something had been troubling her. But the truth was he was no longer sure what he felt for Rose. I'm an all or nothing person, he realised, and I can't go through what Rose put me through again. Anna is right, I've got to forget her and get on with my own life. He hadn't realised how hard it would be to remain friends. Better never to see Rose again. 'Please stay. I want you to.'

She nearly weakened. Jack was such a decent man and so good-looking it would have been easy to give in. No matter what he believes, I know different, she thought, recalling his expression when she said Rose's name. You can't hide what you feel, Jack. 'No. Not now. Give me a ring next weekend when you've had time to think over what I've said. I really like you, Jack. I think you know that, but if our relationship's going anywhere I need to know where I stand.' She picked up her leather coat and bag. 'And I'm sorry about the food, but I really couldn't eat it now.'

Jack nodded. He went to the door with her. 'Shall I walk you home?'

'No. I'll be fine. Thanks, anyway.'

He watched her make her way down the road. She hadn't far to go and it wasn't late or he would have insisted.

Closing the door, he went to the phone. Had Rose already made that call? Was it too late for him to see her? And do I really want to? he asked himself. 'Bloody women,' he said as he picked up the receiver. 'Have you rung Camborne yet?' he asked when Rose answered.

'No.'

'Why not?'

'I was just about to. We needed some time to get our thoughts in order.'

'Then wait until I get there.'

'But I thought . . .' She stopped. About to mention Anna, she could not ask what had taken place to cause Jack to change his mind.

'I'll be there in a few minutes.'

He unhooked a fleece-lined stone-coloured jacket from the peg in the hall and went out to the car. A half moon hung over the bay; its reflection was distorted in the ripples of the sea, as blurred as his feelings about the two females in his life. I'm not on duty, I'm going as a friend, he reminded himself, knowing that Rose's find would have to be reported via official channels. He was confused. Anna seemed to know him better than he knew himself.

There wasn't room in the drive for his car. Behind Rose's Metro was another he did not recognise. He parked in the lay-by across the road and, hands in his pockets against the keen, freshening wind, walked up to the house and tapped on the kitchen window. The light was on. Dishes cluttered the draining-board, more dishes than a single person would have used.

The hall door opened and Rose walked across the kitchen. She wore jeans and boots and a cream, drop-shouldered shirt in a thick material. She looks so young, he thought, so childlike. But he knew her size was partly responsible. Her petite figure was that of a teenage girl.

'I'm glad you came,' Rose said as soon as she opened the door. 'I'd rather talk to you than a stranger. We're in the sitting room.'

Miranda and Joel eyed Jack nervously as the introductions were made. They were not sure if they had committed a crime by breaking into the lock-up but Mrs Trevelyan seemed unconcerned.

'Do you want a drink, or coffee?' Rose asked.

He had seen the wine bottle. One wouldn't hurt. 'Thanks. Then you'd better tell me again what happened this afternoon.'

Rose did so, explaining how it had been her idea to take a look at the place. Jack hid a smile as he pictured the three disparate people before him acting like burglars.

'It's definitely the bag your father packed on the day before you moved?' he asked Miranda.

'Yes. I touched it, I'm afraid.'

Jack didn't think it would yield many clues if it had been left in the damp for all that time. 'It doesn't matter. I'll get someone over there. We'll need to speak to your family, of course, and we'll need statements from the three of you.'

'Will we get into trouble?' Joel wanted to know.

'I very much doubt it. Where can you be reached in the morning?'

Joel told him that Miranda was staying the night at his house. He was relieved, they could face the questions together and Miranda wouldn't have to face her mother and aunt until later. 'Can we go now?'

Jack saw that the boy had had enough. He nodded. 'Don't leave the house, though, not until someone's been to see you.'

'Thank you for the lunch, Rose. We really enjoyed it.'

'It was my pleasure, Joel.' It seemed more like days than hours since they had eaten it and there were still the dishes to wash.

'May I use the phone?' Jack asked.

'Of course.' Rose saw her guests out and waited until the car had reversed down the drive before returning to Jack. 'Thanks for coming. The pair of them are worried sick. I know you're taking this seriously now.'

'Yes, but it still doesn't mean anything's happened to him.'

Rose explained about the boat. 'There'd have to be a record, wouldn't there?'

'He might have sold it privately before he left. What puzzles me is why he didn't get rid of the boathouse. I suppose it's possible he thought he might continue to use it but then I'd assume the boat would still be there. Let's hope we find out.'

174

Rose looked at the empty wine bottle. They had been quite abstemious throughout the day because she had been aware that Joel was under-age and Miranda had the car. 'I'll get another drink,' she said, knowing what would be going through Jack's mind. Or did she? What had he said to Anna and how must she be feeling to have been ditched for his ex-lover?

'I hope I didn't spoil your evening,' she said when she returned with the open bottle.

Jack shrugged. It had been Anna's decision to leave. Had he tried hard enough to stop her? He didn't know. But he was not prepared to discuss his relationship, if it still was one, with Rose. 'So let's hear it all. Right from the beginning, not just from today.'

Rose told him, even mentioning the electric freezer at the house on Bodmin Moor. 'They all seem to suspect each other from what I can gather. It's a very strange set-up,' she concluded.

'Well, we might get to the bottom of it when we've spoken to the sisters. Have you heard any more from the one who attacked you?'

'No. And I don't particularly want to. She isn't going to be very pleased when she knows Miranda and Joel were here and that I was responsible for finding Frank's bag.'

'You can take care of yourself, Rose. You always make a point of telling me that.'

She blushed. The criticism, if it was one, was accurate. 'How is it you now feel free to interview Louisa and Wendy? I mean, you still don't seem certain a crime's been committed,' she asked in order to change the subject.

He grinned. 'Apart from a touch of breaking and

entering? Well, Roger Penhaligon was on the phone again the other week, which proves he is still concerned about his brother-in-law, and now his clothes and personal papers have been found, we have reason to be suspicious. You have to accept that we might be pissing into the wind. Jordan could've dumped his things at the last minute not wishing to take any reminders with him. He might even have forgotten where he put his passport.'

Rose stood up. 'At least you're looking into it. I'm convinced there's something not quite right.'

'When aren't you?'

She had imagined that the conversation was over, that, business done, Jack would want to get back to Anna. When he made no move to get up himself she sat down again. 'Don't let me detain you if you have to go,' she said.

'There's no rush. Any chance of a refill?' He held out the empty glass.

'Of course.'

'Anna had to leave. Something cropped up.' He had not meant to bring her into the conversation. 'I'd invited her over for a meal but we didn't get to eat it.'

'Is this your way of telling me you're hungry?' Had Anna left because of her telephone call? If that was the case the relationship was already on rocky ground.

'Actually, I'm starving.'

'Then you're in luck. How about a roast beef and salad sandwich?'

'Ideal. Do you need any help?' He followed her to the kitchen anyway. 'Motive,' he said, 'that's the one thing that's lacking in all this. Louisa is well provided for, as is Wendy.'

'Jealousy? It's a powerful emotion.'

'Possibly. But why wait for so long? No, if he hasn't simply done a bunk then it's more likely your theory is right. There was an argument that went badly wrong and something happened to Jordan. But in that case, tell me, Rose, where the hell is the body?'

She turned to face him, the buttery knife in her hands. 'In the sea? Maybe that's why the boat's missing. One or both of them took him out in it and sank it.'

'Oh, yes. I can just see a woman of a certain age lugging a fully grown man, a dead weight at that, down to the lock-up or whatever and taking the boat out. And how would she or they have got back?'

'It was summer. The boat would've been moored somewhere. And there'd have been an inflatable dinghy surely.'

'Which would also have to be disposed of.'

Rose sliced two thick pieces of beef and laid them on the bread. Lettuce and tomato followed. The second slice she spread liberally with mustard. 'There you are. There's more if you're still hungry.'

'Thank you.' Jack took the plate and began to eat, standing by the table.

'There's another possibility. Suicide.'

'Again, why?' he asked, wiping mustard from his lower lip.

'Why does anyone kill themselves?'

'No note, no suggestion of it really.'

'No.' But another idea had occurred to Rose. She would keep it to herself for the moment. Jack believed her to be fanciful enough as it was.

Watching him eat, quite at ease even if he had chosen

to remain on his feet, she realised how quickly they had slipped back into their old ways. They were discussing this as equals and there was no animosity. Jack was taking her seriously and respecting her views.

'Mm, delish,' he said, bolting down the last mouthful.

'Another?' He nodded. With her back to him she sliced more bread. 'What were you cooking?'

'Pasta.'

'Then it's ruined. I'm sorry.'

'This more than makes up for it.'

He obviously wasn't going to be drawn. Rose wanted to know why Anna had decided to go home early but it wasn't something she could ask him outright. She knew he was watching her and suspected he might be laughing. Was she that easy to read? To hell with it, why shouldn't she say what was on her mind. 'I take it you're both still coming on Christmas Eve?'

'Mm. I'm looking forward to meeting your parents again. They're nice people.' He wouldn't admit that Anna would not be coming.

'They'll be here on Monday. Here's your sandwich. Look, Jack, the portrait, that's when it all started really, the day they changed their minds. Surely that means they've got something to hide. Wendy, at least, certainly didn't want me to become aware that Miranda was back.'

'We'll be having a long talk with that young lady. Has it occurred to you that if a crime has been committed she could be the guilty party?'

It hadn't. And now Jack had said it, it was a more realistic reason for Miranda to have disappeared than any she had given.

'And the boy. Those two seemed unusually close. Maybe whatever they know binds them together.'

Rose started to clear up the lunchtime mess. Yes, she had been suspicious, had been looking for a mystery where none might exist, but even she hadn't suspected the younger members of the family. And I've only got Miranda's word that Wendy was alone with Frank on that morning, she realised.

Jack didn't leave until half past ten. They sat by the fire going over all that Rose had discovered but still none of it made any sense. 'Will you let me know what happens?' she asked when he said it was time to make a move.

'Yes, of course. You realise you'll have to make a statement, too?'

'So you said.'

'Only concerning the lock-up. Facts, Rose, not what your imagination dictates.'

He had to do it. Just when they were getting on so well, he had to have a final dig. 'There don't seem to be many facts, Jack. Perhaps if someone had listened to Roger Penhaligon when Frank and Miranda went missing things may have been different. Goodnight.'

He inclined his head but did not speak. But Rose knew that this time he was really laughing at her. She slammed the kitchen door and ran hot water into the bowl. She would vent her anger on the dishes.

CHAPTER THIRTEEN

Jack decided to speak to the sisters himself. He rang the number Rose had given him and asked if it was convenient for him to come even though it was a Sunday morning.

'Yes,' Louisa told him. 'We'll be here.' She had sounded business-like but not as if she had anything to hide.

A female detective constable accompanied him. During the journey they discussed what they knew. They had learnt little from the holdall, which had been removed from the lock-up and was being held as evidence – of what, he still had no idea. It had contained enough clothes for three or four days, Jordan's passport and his driving licence. What puzzled Jack was why the latter two items were there at all. Surely they would have been packed safely along with all the family documents? And if the bag was meant to be hidden, why place it somewhere where it was likely to be found? Was it supposed to be found, so that the man would be assumed to be dead?

They had a clear run and reached the old farmhouse early. Louisa Jordan answered the door. Her appearance, and that of the interior of the house, surprised Jack.

Tasteful, he decided, and none of it had come cheaply. They were shown into the large room at the back where a fire blazed in the grate. The day was dull and lifeless but the view must be wonderful when the sun shone.

'My sister, Wendy,' Louisa said as she opened the door. 'Would you like some coffee, Inspector? Constable?'

'Not for me, I'm fine, thanks,' Jack said. DC Maunder shook her head.

'Then please sit down and tell us why you feel the need to speak to us.'

Louisa chose to sit next to her sister on the settee. Jack wondered if this was to put on a show of solidarity as he took a seat by the fire. Susan Maunder took a chair out of sight of the sisters. She was aware she would not be required to say anything, she was there as a chaperone more than anything else. 'Your brother, Roger Penhaligon, has been in touch with us. It seems he's still not satisfied with the way in which your husband disappeared. Can you shed any light on it?'

Louisa sighed as if she was tired of going over it. 'None whatsoever. As far as I was aware we were moving here. We'd packed, everything was ready. Frank gave no indication whatsoever that he wasn't coming with me. I'd spent the morning in Penzance; when I returned he'd left. His bag was gone and I've never heard from him since. Later, Wendy sold up and joined me.'

'You didn't consider contacting us at the time?'

'No. I knew my husband. He was a selfish man, it was not untypical of him, leaving me to pick up the pieces. I truly believed he used the move as his chance to escape. Miranda was set to leave home, I thought he felt he no

181

longer had any responsibilities as far as we were concerned, and this house was paid for and in my name.'

'Did you often have to do so, pick up the pieces?'

Louisa bit her lip. 'Financially, yes, on several occasions.'

'I have to ask, was there another woman?'

Wendy seemed about to speak but shook her head and remained silent.

'There were several over the years. Nothing I considered to be serious. Not until then. I've always assumed he'd finally met someone he really wanted to be with.'

'Mrs Jordan, if that was the case why not tell you? Why not apply for a divorce in the ordinary way?'

'I really don't know.'

'We've found his bag.'

'Pardon?'

'The bag he packed on the day he left.'

'How could you have? And how do you know it's his?'

'It contains his passport and driving licence.'

She stared at the fire as she took this information in. 'Am I allowed to know where you found it?'

She's flustered, Jack thought, but not as much as her sister. Wendy was pale, one hand to her throat. 'In the lock-up where he kept the boat.'

'But I thought he'd sold the garage. He told me he was going to.'

'Apparently not. Nor do we know what's happened to the boat. Have you any idea?'

'No. And I don't understand any of this. Why on earth did you go to the lock-up?'

Jack hesitated before answering. 'It was your daughter

who led us to it, along with her cousin.'

Several seconds of silence followed this remark. 'Was Mrs Trevelyan involved in any way?' Wendy asked.

'She was with them, yes.' He had not meant to bring Rose into this but he saw that his reply had rattled the women further and that might not be a bad thing.

'Why?'

'She had invited them to lunch. Somehow or other the subject came up and they decided to take a look.' He hoped the sisters wouldn't ask how they had got in.

'It seems to me everyone is more concerned about Frank's whereabouts than I am myself. But you were right to come here. It does seem odd, him leaving his passport. Inspector Pearce, are you saying you think that something may have happened to him?'

'In view of the concern of the rest of your family, we have to consider that possibility.'

'I see.'

Jack studied her. She was visibly shaken, as if the idea had never occurred to her, yet Rose believed all three women were of the same opinion and each suspected the other.

'Could it be that he went out in his boat, one last trip before he sold it, and got careless because he couldn't bear the thought of losing it?' Louisa suggested.

'At this stage anything's possible, but why would he need to sell it at all? It's not that far from here to the sea.' Over the previous year and a bit there had been no sighting of any wreckage matching the description of the boat which Miranda had supplied, no body washed up on the shore, but he might have gone down in an area where the tides

183

were relentless, where the boat or the body would never be recovered. Even so, the wife's lack of concern at the time was strange. Maybe the boat had been sabotaged, a small hole made in its base. No, he thought, not if Rose was right and it was moored in the harbour or elsewhere. It would have sunk before he got to it. 'Where was the boat when you moved?'

'If he hadn't sold it, the *Louisa* would have been in Penzance harbour. Unless, of course, he took her with him.'

'If your husband was dead, how would you stand financially, Mrs Jordan?'

'That's an impertinent question, Inspector, but if it pleases you, I'll answer it. Nothing would change. This house and its contents are mine. Money slipped through Frank's hands like water. He had far more to gain by my death. We are not divorced, I assume half of everything would be his.'

True, Jack realised. But if Jordan was profligate and had wanted a divorce he, too, would be aware of how he stood financially. Had he asked his wife for one? Had she refused and decided to take matters into her own hands? Rose had been right, there was something these women didn't want him to know. 'Your daughter's not with you at present?'

'No. We were expecting her back this morning. She's obviously prolonged her visit.'

Which meant Miranda had not been in contact with them, had not warned them or confided in them. Was she afraid to return? Jack knew that two officers had gone to interview her and Joel first thing that morning. She could have made it back by now. 'I think we'll leave it at that, for the time being,' he added, letting them know he was not completely satisfied.

'We could have told you all this over the telephone,' Louisa said as she stood.

Jack made no response. He would not have been able to read their body language over the telephone. They were guilty of something but whether it was murder or not he had no idea. He had had no excuse to ask about the deep freeze. Only Rose could have told him it was there and they would not have thanked her for that. He stood. DC Maunder followed suit and they left the house. 'A strange pair,' she commented when they were in the car.

'You can say that again.' How on earth does Rose meet these people? he asked himself as he started the engine. His mind on the unsatisfactory interview he failed to notice the beauty of the countryside. But beside him, his companion took it all in. Like the Inspector she had once been transferred but found she could not wait to return to her native Cornwall again.

Back at the station Jack sat down to read the statements provided by Miranda and Joel.

Half an hour later he knew they contained no more than what they had said the previous evening. Which led him back to Anna. He still had no idea what he would say to her at the end of the week or how he could explain to Rose the reason she was not accompanying him to the party on Christmas Eve.

Rose was in St Ives still awaiting inspiration as far as a present for her parents was concerned. By mid-morning on Sunday she had given up and was sipping coffee in one of the numerous cafes. She had forgotten so many of the shops would be open that day. It had clouded over but it was warm inside and the smell of freshly baked pasties filled the air. They'll be here tomorrow, she thought, I'll have to find something.

She left the cafe and started again, strolling slowly around the ancient, narrow streets of one of the most visited fishing ports in England. Surely she'd find something suitable in one of the small shops. At one time horses and carts had drawn thousands of tons of pilchards through those narrow streets and up the steep and winding hills. These days those same streets were thronged with tourists in the summer, but they were no quieter back in the 1800s and during the first half of the twentieth century. Rose recalled an eyewitness account she had read in the museum in a street called Wheal Dream about one occasion when a hundred thousand hogsheads were in St Ives Bay at one time. A hogshead held three thousand fish. Trumpets had roared to alert the fishermen that the pilchards were coming into the bay. A network of 'seins' was spread across the water and boats span about like a regatta. The women would have been waiting to pack and carry the fish. Women. Rose's thoughts reverted to Miranda and Joel. Jack, or someone, would have spoken to them by now and, presumably, to Louisa and Wendy Maybe he'd ring her tonight, maybe he'd even call in. She stopped. There in a window was a black woollen cardigan with silver threads running through it. Just the sort of thing her mother loved. She went inside and bought it.

Inspiration struck again. In a men's clothing shop she saw a hat. A sort of trilby in shades of dark green and tan. A small feather was stuck in its band. It was almost identical to the battered one her father wore. Fortunately she knew his hat size. I just hope he won't be upset when Mum insists he throws the old one out, she thought while she waited for it to be wrapped in tissue paper and placed in a bag.

With a clear conscience she drove home. There was no present for Jack this year, neither did she expect one in return. The small gifts she had bought for her friends were already wrapped ready to be handed out on Christmas Eve.

There was plenty to do in the house and she had adjusted to the fact that no painting would be done until after Christmas. She would miss it, but return to it fresher for the break.

The red light on the answering-machine remained glowing steadily. No one had telephoned. Good. She pulled the hoover out from under the stairs and got down to some serious housework.

By six thirty there was nothing more to be done other than to cook herself a meal and relax. And then the telephone did ring. Jack, she thought as she hurried to answer it.

'Mrs Trevelyan, it's Louisa. Is Miranda with you by any chance?'

'No. She was here yesterday and I understood she was staying with Joel last night.' There was no point in pretending she didn't know, no point in more deceit. Jack would have explained the situation to them anyway.

'Ah. Then she's probably still there. We had a detective here this morning. It was to do with you finding Frank's bag. What's going on, Mrs Trevelyan? Why are you so concerned with our family?'

How could she answer? Not by telling the truth, but nor could she drop Miranda in it. 'I think your daughter's still worried about her father. She wanted to see if the boat was still there. She didn't believe he would sell it.'

'You broke in?'

'I—'

'There's no need to answer. You must have done. Frank had the only set of keys.'

If that was true then only Frank could have put the bag there. Wrong. If Frank had been killed whoever killed him could easily have taken the keys. But why leave it there where there was a chance of it being found? I'm sick of this, Rose thought wishing she had taken Barry's advice and kept out of it from the beginning, wishing, in fact, she had never been commissioned to paint that portrait.

'I think we should talk. Will you be free tomorrow morning?'

'I'm expecting visitors after lunch.'

'I'll come to you. I don't expect you to drive up here. I don't suppose what we have to say will take up too much of your time.'

'Why not talk now?'

'I'd prefer to do it face to face. If it isn't convenient, please say so and I'll make it another time.'

Rose swore under her breath. She knew she could not miss out on the opportunity. 'That's fine. As early as you like.'

'I'll try and be there by nine thirty.'

No sooner had she hung up than Jack rang. Some days were like that, all or nothing.

'There's something going on,' he said without preamble, 'but I'm damned if I know what it is. We've searched the

188

bag. There's nothing in there to give us a clue and there was nothing else in the lock-up.'

'What did you make of my ex-clients?'

'They were hiding something.'

'Did you mention the portrait, did you ask them the real reason why they changed their minds?'

'No. This was just an informal chat.'

'But what are you going to do?'

'You tell me, Rose. It's not as if we have a body.'

'You don't need one to conduct a murder inquiry.'

'I do happen to be aware of that. Look, I've had a hard day. Let's leave it until the 24th. We can catch up then.'

Not with Anna around, she thought, unaware that Anna would not now be coming. 'Okay. See you soon.' She had hung up before she realised she had not mentioned Louisa's call.

Her parents would have eaten lunch on the way – they always took the drive down from Gloucestershire slowly, setting off early and stopping at least twice on the way – therefore Rose had nothing to do until their arrival, but she still resented the fact that Louisa would be taking up part of the morning which she could have put to better use in her attic workroom.

However, Louisa arrived promptly at nine twenty-five. Unlike her sister she came to the front of the house, shaking rain from her coat as Rose tugged at the swollen door. 'Thank you for agreeing to see me,' Louisa said as she followed Rose into the sitting room.

'Coffee?' she asked, thinking she was seeing a fair amount of the whole family recently.

'If it's no trouble.'

Prepared in advance, the pot was full. Rose laid out some biscuits and carried the tray across the hallway. Louisa, like everyone who came to the house, stood in the window admiring the view. 'I miss it,' she said, turning to Rose. 'I didn't realise how much a part of me it was. Still, I love the new house and I don't regret moving. It's so unbelievably peaceful.'

Rose said nothing. She would allow a few minutes of small talk then ask why she was really there.

'I'll get to the point, Rose. I feel I owe you an explanation regarding the portrait. Miranda had gone, we didn't know where. We both love her, Wendy and I, we love her very much. I had no idea she'd come home as she did, no idea why she left, really, other than what she said in her note. She obviously wasn't as happy at home as I'd always believed. We wanted it done for her, we were going to leave it to her, something to remember us by. When she came home it no longer seemed important, not when she was there in the flesh. It might sound odd to you, in fact, I'm sure it does, but that's the truth.'

Partly, Rose thought, but not all of it. She leant over to pour the coffee and handed a cup to Louisa. 'Why not finish it anyway?'

'Maybe, maybe sometime in the future. Things have changed, you see.'

'I want you to know I didn't deliberately become involved with your family. As I told you before, it was pure coincidence that I met Joel and, consequently, his parents. And Miranda came to me, I didn't seek her out.'

'I know that, she told me. What did she want to speak to you about?'

'About Joel.'

'Not about her father?'

'No, not initially. That subject only came up on Saturday. She was worried, she still can't understand why he left.'

'No, but Miranda didn't know him as I did. They rubbed along together, but Frank loved her more than she did him. She would never allow herself to get to know him properly. For all his faults he had a good side. He was an exciting man to be with, he always made you feel alive. He took risks.' She shrugged. 'Maybe he took one too many.'

The past tense, Rose thought. Was it relevant or simply a figure of speech because she hadn't seen him for such a long time? 'What sort of risks?'

'Financial ones. Sometimes they paid off, latterly they didn't. The police seem to think something may have happened to him.'

'Do you?'

'I don't know what to think, Rose. Perhaps he was in deeper than I thought and he killed himself.' She shook her head. 'No. I just can't see Frank doing that, he wasn't the type.'

There was no type, as Louisa put it. Many families believed suicide was out of the question when people they knew had taken their own lives. It was a possibility. But if so, why were the women so unprepared to be honest? Why hadn't anyone made a fuss at the time?

'And now, all this, with the police.' Louisa pulled a tissue from her handbag and wiped her eyes. The bag was open on the floor. A stamped envelope caught Rose's eye. 'If only he'd written, or left a note. You probably think I was callous not going to the police at the time, but there hasn't been a day when I've not hoped to hear something. I've always loved that man, I still do.'

'What would've happened if he had come back and found Wendy living with you?'

'I'd have asked her to leave. Frank would never have put up with that.'

Rose poured more coffee. Nothing the woman said rang true. Why allow her sister to move in so quickly when she may have had to ask her to leave again? It was hardly fair on Wendy who, she assumed, was unaware of what her fate would have been.

Louisa accepted her refilled cup. 'Thank you. What I can't understand is why the police are interested now. They didn't bother when Roger initially contacted them, any more than they did about Miranda.'

Whom you didn't report missing either, Rose thought. I wonder why that was, when you claim she was a much-beloved daughter. 'Louisa, we seem to be covering old ground here. Was there anything in particular you wanted to tell or ask me?'

'Now that I'm here, I don't know. I just had a feeling you could help me, put my mind at rest somehow. I think Miranda believed that, too.'

And in a way I did. We broke into the lock-up and found Frank Jordan's holdall. 'What did Wendy think of Frank?'

Louisa looked up, startled by the question. 'Oh, they got on reasonably well. Frank always considered her to be a bit stuffy. She considered him to be – well, larger than life, I suppose. She felt he didn't treat me well, but she knew nothing of our marriage. Frank may have lived the life of a playboy, if that term is still in use, but he always came back to me. I always believed it was me he loved.'

'Even more of a reason for reporting him missing, I would've thought.' Rose was thinking aloud but she heard Louisa's slight gasp.

'I think I'd better go now. I just hope all this blows over quickly. I've got Miranda back, I daren't dream that Frank might return. If he did we might all have a chance of being happy again.' She picked up her bag.

Rose handed her her coat which she had draped over a chair near the fire. She's told me nothing, she thought as she showed her out. I have no idea why she came here. Unless it was to find out how much I know. 'Goodbye,' she said. 'I hope you have a good Christmas.'

'Thank you. You, too.'

Rose closed the door and stood in the hall for several minutes. Louisa Jordan had gone out of her way to convince Rose that her marriage had been happy. But why unless she really had killed him? I'll think about it later. I'll prepare the evening meal and then I'll think about the reason she might have had that letter in her bag. 'If only he'd written' Louisa had said. Well, maybe he had.

CHAPTER FOURTEEN

Louisa was driving too fast. Easing her foot off the accelerator, she rotated her neck to relieve the tension. It had been a mistake to visit the Trevelyan woman. She had hoped to learn what Miranda and Joel had said to her, to learn of their suspicions, for she was sure they existed. But she had probably only aroused Rose's curiosity further.

The future she dreamt of lay ahead of her but her plans had been put on hold until after Christmas. Louisa wanted to meet Michael to discover if he and Miranda had a chance of making a go of it. She also wanted to see if her daughter had any plans to take up her university place. It wasn't too late, Louisa had already made inquiries. She sighed. And there was Wendy to contend with. There would be a scene, it was only to be expected. In retrospect she realised that loneliness was the reason she had agreed to Wendy's suggestion that she join her at the house. Loneliness, and a fear that she might have been deceived. The arrangement had worked although Louisa became uncomfortable with it after the first few months.

Miranda had returned the previous evening with no excuses as to why she hadn't telephoned to let them know she'd be late. She had been subdued until Louisa had reassured her that she knew where she had been and what had taken place. 'The police spoke to us too,' she had said. 'A man named Inspector Pearce. It was concerning your father's boat.'

'We met him. Joel and I,' Miranda had responded. Louisa had noticed the slight hesitation before mentioning her cousin's name. 'He's a friend of Rose's.'

He would be, Louisa thought as she turned into the lane which led to the house. It was still muddy and shallow puddles filled the ruts. The dirty water splashed the sides of the car as she drove through them. But the rain had stopped and the sky was clearing. She would take a walk, get Miranda to go with her and hopefully persuade Wendy to stay at home. She had hardly left them alone for a second. With a look of determination on her face she entered the house. Rose Trevelyan was not the only one with a stubborn streak.

Rose's parents arrived just before four o'clock. It was not dark but it soon would be, although the shortest day had passed. Halfway through their journey the rain had cleared. They had followed the setting sun westwards, the sky altering colour dramatically. From a pale blue with banks of cloud it was suddenly lit with orange fingers which turned the clouds pink and then purple with the first signs of dusk. Now, as they stood in Rose's drive, the purple was deepening and lights began to come on throughout the village below them.

Evelyn and Arthur Forbes were delighted to see their daughter, their only child. They were a small family and Rose would be the last in the line. They each hugged her in turn. 'You look tired, Rose,' Evelyn said as they stepped into the warmth of the kitchen. 'I hope you haven't been overdoing things on our behalf. We told you we'd settle for a quiet Christmas.'

'No, I'm fine.' Rose smiled. She was weary. There had been the buffet and the Christmas dinner to organise coupled with her concern over Miranda and her peculiar family. Curiosity could be quite tiring. And Jack. Mostly it was Jack, of course. 'Heavens, what on earth's in there?'

Arthur was placing a large cardboard box on the table. His battered trilby was at an angle on his head. Rose wondered once more whether he would be able to bear to part with it.

'Presents, and one or two other goodies. You have a rummage while we go and unpack.' He picked up the small bag which contained their things.

Rose put the kettle on then lifted out several perfectly wrapped packages with her name on. She could not guess at their contents. There was another small one for Laura and one for Barry. How thoughtful they are, Rose was thinking. Tonight she and her mother would decorate the small fir tree she had bought to stand in the bay of the window. It was a family tradition that it was left until the 23rd although, since David's death, Rose had rarely bothered with a tree. The presents would go under it.

'Very nice,' she said to herself as she removed bottles of port and brandy and one of lovage. There was also a ripe

196

Stilton and a large box of chocolates. Rose began to feel in more of a festive mood. Every year it seemed harder to get into the spirit of Christmas. For no reason at all a particular scene came into her head, one she was sure she had noticed recently. 'Yes, that's it. Bodmin Moor.'

'Pardon?' Her father stood in the doorway scratching his head where his hatband had left a mark.

'My next masterpiece. I've just decided where to set it.'

'Ah.' And there would be a very good reason for that. Arthur wondered what relevance Bodmin Moor had to her present life. He was sure he would find out even if he had to ask Jack Pearce.

Rose was making them tea when her mother joined them. She had changed her clothes and brushed her hair. Yes, it was a good idea. The moor wasn't all bleak. There were areas where trees grew and wild flowers bloomed in the spring. Maybe she would find a farmhouse, not Louisa's, and use it as the focal point. Maybe she could find one where, from a distance, it was framed by the branches of trees with wilder scenery, maybe an outcrop of rocks, as the backdrop. If I can bear the cold I could start in the New Year when there might be snow on the higher ground. What contrasts of colour I could capture if I was blessed by a bright blue winter sky, she thought as she placed the sugar bowl on the tray.

Evelyn and Arthur followed their daughter into the sitting room where she had lit a fire. As Rose bent to pour the tea her father thought anew how much his daughter resembled his wife even though Evelyn's hair had lost much of its vibrant colour and was threaded liberally with grey which she made no attempt to conceal. It fell just below her ears and was held back with a velvet band, a style she had not altered for years. It suited her and somehow managed not to appear dated. Arthur hid a smile as he wondered how the two women viewed him.

Without meaning to, Rose began to explain about the two sisters and Joel and his family 'His parents are away at the moment otherwise I'd have got them more involved and got myself out of it all.'

Highly unlikely, Arthur thought, but did not say. He caught his wife's eye and winked. Jack'll sort her out, he thought. But it was Evelyn who brought up his name. 'And what does Jack have to say about all this?'

'Ah, yes. Jack. I think you ought to know that he's found himself a woman. Her name's Anna. I haven't met her yet, but he's bringing her along tomorrow.'

Evelyn bit her lip. She was extremely disappointed. Jack had seemed ideal for Rose, the perfect counterfoil to her temperament. But Rose was stubborn and it was no use interfering. And if she was heartbroken she was hiding it well. Evelyn looked at her over the rim of her teacup. Rose's hand shook only a little as she replaced her cup on its saucer. So that's how the land lies. She is upset but she refuses to admit it. It was time to change the subject. 'Shall we have a walk before dinner?'

'That's a very good idea. I haven't been out of the house all day.' It already seemed as if Louisa's early morning visit had taken place in a different era. 'Unless you want any more tea, why don't we set off now?'

'No, we're fine. Would you get my coat, please, Arthur?'

He hoisted himself out of his chair. He would have been content to sit there and read the *Cornishman*, the local weekly paper, while the two women caught up on gossip. But he had been in the car for many hours, the walk would do him good.

When they were ready Rose locked up and they left the house. 'Which way?' she asked as they made their way down the drive.

'Towards Mousehole, I think,' Evelyn decided. 'We can have a pre-dinner drink at the . . . my word, look at all the traffic.' A steady stream of cars was headed towards Mousehole and quite a lot were travelling in the opposite direction towards Newlyn.

'How stupid of me,' Rose said. 'I've been so busy, I'd forgotten. We'll walk there by all means, but we'll never get served. It's Tom Bowcock's night.'

'Of course it is.' Evelyn knew the story well. Each year on 23rd December the Ship Inn provided enormous star-gazey pies in remembrance of Tom who, many years before, had braved the raging seas in order to catch fish to save the village from starvation and had succeeded. 'And the lights, as well.'

'Well, we always like to look at them if we're here at Christmas,' Arthur added, although that had only been on a couple of occasions. Coachloads came from far and wide to see them. Some were set high in the hills, others lined the harbour walls, some floated on the water when the tide was in and sat on the sand when it wasn't.

They set off along the narrow footpath, sometimes walking in single file, but not often since the new cycle path had been built. There were other people on foot. Parking was always difficult, tonight it would probably be impossible.

'Oh, look, Arthur.' Evelyn had stopped to look at the bay. It was a clear night and the moon was nearly three-quarters full. Its reflection shimmered in the sea. Below, to the left, the Newlyn Christmas lights could be seen. Ahead, the bulk of St Michael's Mount protruded starkly from the bay and was dimly outlined against the coastline behind it. It was a magical sight. 'It's always so beautiful, no matter when you look at it,' Evelyn commented.

'I know.' Rose was keenly aware that she would never be able to live happily anywhere else. They continued on their way in silence.

It was a clear but not cold night, not even chilly enough for Evelyn to have brought her gloves, and, as they walked, they became warmer still. Within twenty-five minutes they had reached their destination. Rose could have made it in less time but her parents, although both still highly active, had slowed down a little.

People were milling around the harbour walls of the quaint village and many of the small craft shops were open. Flashbulbs popped and video cameras whirred. Noise and laughter spilt out of the Ship and customers stood drinking on the narrow road because there were no pavements. 'It's busier than on a summer's day,' Arthur commented as he stepped out of the way of a group of people. Evelyn didn't hear him; she was watching a couple of cars trying to manoeuvre their way around the hairpin bend between pedestrians. How the local buses coped was beyond her.

She had seen them reverse up and back and swing around the corner for their return trip to Penzance without mishap.

'If you fancy a drink we could try the Coastguards,' Rose suggested. They had passed it before their descent into the village. It was a large pub with a view of the bay and St Clement's Island from the recently added conservatory. It would be very busy from the overspill but they'd have more chance of finding a space at the bar and getting served.

They made their way back up the hill via tiny alleyways lined with picturesque cottages outside which were pots of plants, some still in bloom. As lovely as it was Rose had no desire to live in Mousehole. She disliked crowds and too many outsiders had now moved in. Newlyn was a proper working village where the fishermen still fished and the fish market operated.

Once inside the pub Arthur managed to squeeze to the bar where he ordered their drinks. Rose waved to some people she knew but there was no chance of speaking to them, not without shoving through the crowd. 'If you want another we'll have it in the Star,' Rose said. 'There's a bus in ten minutes, it'll drop us right outside if we ask the driver.'

'Suits me,' Arthur said as he swallowed the last of his pint.

The bus passed them on its way down to the village as they waited to cross the road. Minutes later it reappeared and they got on, along with several other people. Cars lined one side of the road way beyond the boundary of Mousehole and more people were walking towards the lights. Newlyn would be empty by comparison.

'Whatever's that?' Evelyn asked, pointing out of the

201

window of the bus. A brightly painted, strange-looking vessel had moored in the bay.

Rose peered across in front of her mother. 'It's a lightship,' she said knowledgeably. 'It won't be much of a Christmas for the crew.' But yours will be one of the best, she decided, Jack or no Jack.

The bus trundled down past Rose's house and on towards Newlyn. Once they reached the Strand Rose stood and spoke to the driver who obliged by pulling in directly outside the Star. Inside it was quieter than usual but there were several locals who were known to Rose and who recognised her parents. They chatted to some of them. Rose glanced at her watch. It was almost seven. It was time to go, there was the tree to see to, the meal to cook and tomorrow would be busier still. She half regretted having organised the party with Christmas Day to follow. A couple of the fishermen shook hands with Arthur and Evelyn as they left.

They took it slowly back up the hill. Arthur watched television while Rose and Evelyn decorated the tree. It didn't take long, it was only three feet tall. Rose then cooked their meal. Evelyn's offer to help was refused. 'It's all ready, it won't take me long, but you can lay the table if you like.'

'Rose, about Jack.' Evelyn stood with a handful of cutlery. The walk had brought colour to her naturally pale complexion. In checked wool trousers, a thick cream shirt and a matching knitted jacket she looked elegant and younger than her years.

'What about him?' Rose prodded the vegetables. The plates were already warming in the bottom of the oven. She didn't want to turn around.

'Do you miss him?'

The monkfish was cut into strips. Rose put it into the olive oil and butter she had heated and quickly forked it over until it was opaque on all sides. She turned up the heat and added a good dash of Pernod which sizzled as it hit the pan. Its liquorice aroma filled the room. 'Yes, I do, actually,' she replied, keeping her back towards her mother.

'But you asked him to come tomorrow?'

'I couldn't not. It would have seemed churlish.'

Or shown him how much you minded, Evelyn thought. 'And you say you don't know this Anna?'

'No.'

'I'm sorry, love, if you'd rather not talk about it.'

Rose shrugged. It hurt, there was no denying that, but there was no point in avoiding the subject. 'It's okay, I really don't mind. Would you tell Dad it's ready?'

'Of course.'

Over the meal they caught up on each other's news and gossip. Her parents were thrilled with Rose's success with her oils, but disappointed that her first attempt at a serious portrait had been abandoned. No more mention of Jack was made that night, for which Rose was grateful.

The following day there was no time for Rose to dwell on any of the matters which were troubling her. As soon as their makeshift breakfast of tea and toast had been eaten and the dishes cleared away she set about taking the ready prepared food out of the freezer. Her parents, recognising that determined look, the tilt of the chin, said they would take themselves off somewhere and return after lunch. 'We'll probably take a run over to St Ives,'

Arthur said. 'Is there anything you want?'

'No, there can't possibly be,' Rose said, recalling all the shopping she had done over the past few weeks.

Arthur pulled on his hat and bent his tall, lean frame to kiss the top of his daughter's head. 'Are you sure we can't help you with anything?' He felt guilty about leaving her but knew he would be considered in the way.

'Positive.' Once they had left, Rose made up bowls of salad. A presenter on Radio 4 was talking quietly in the background but Rose wasn't really listening, she was wondering where Frank Jordan would be spending Christmas and if his wife would be thinking about him. I no longer have any idea whether he's dead or alive, she realised as she cut radishes into shapes to decorate the cold meats. At least Joel was with friends and Miranda had mentioned a boyfriend who was coming to visit. What would Louisa and Wendy make of another addition to their household?

The next hour or so flew by. During the afternoon Rose and her parents took it in turns to shower and change ready for the evening. At five-thirty, wearing the apple green dress she had worn to the Penhaligons' party, Rose poured their first drink. 'Cheers,' she said raising her glass. 'I'm ready for this.'

'Cheers. And you look lovely,' Arthur said, raising his in response. 'Just like your mother, in fact,' he added, winking at Evelyn who, elegant as usual, was dressed in a coffee-coloured dress and jacket made from shimmering material.

Like the Penhaligons, Rose had invited her guests early because many of them had guests of their own to see to the following day, or small children who would drag them out of bed before daybreak. At six-thirty precisely there was a knock on the kitchen door. Rose stood up. 'No bets on who that is,' she said.

'Doreen Clarke?'

Rose grinned at her mother. 'Spot on.' Doreen thought that if an invitation was for six-thirty, then that was exactly when she ought to arrive.

'Here's the carrot roses,' Doreen said by way of greeting as she thrust an ice-cold polythene bag into Rose's hands.

'Thank you. What would you like to drink?'

'A drop of gin for me, Cyril'll have a beer, won't you, dear?'

Cyril nodded and twisted his cap in his hands. Used to his miner's headgear for so many years, he had taken to wearing the cap after he was made redundant. Doreen always had to remind him to take it off indoors even though he felt undressed without it.

Rose poured their drinks. 'Go on through, my parents are in the sitting room. I shan't be a minute.' She untied the bag and placed the decorative carrot shapes amongst the garnish surrounding the sandwiches, pasties and flans. Every working surface in the kitchen was covered with plates of food; the drinks she had laid out on the table.

'Don't stand there like that, Cyril, you heard what Rose said, let's go and say hello to Arthur and Evelyn.'

Cyril patted Rose's arm as he walked past. He had not spoken a single word since his arrival but Rose knew that once his wife was circulating and he'd had a few more beers, he'd strike up a conversation about gardening with

205

anyone who would listen. He hated socialising, he was only happy in the company of other ex-miners or when tending his vegetables, but he had come to please Doreen whom, despite her tendency to bossiness, he cared about deeply.

The house gradually began to fill up. There was a real mixture of guests: friends, fishermen and their wives, and other artists. Arthur had been put in charge of the CD player. There was no room for dancing and as everyone was far too busy talking to care what they were listening to his choice of music was hardly relevant.

It was seven-thirty before Jack appeared. Rose was in the kitchen but didn't hear his knock because Laura, dressed in a purple Lycra dress which fitted like cling-film, had a group of people laughing loudly. Whatever she was saying was accompanied by extravagant gestures made with the whole of her thin body. Her mass of curls flew wildly around her head. Even though she couldn't hear what was being said Rose laughed too. Laura resembled some African tribal dancer.

'Hello. I brought you these.'

Rose nearly dropped the bottle from which she was replenishing drinks. With shaking hands she screwed the top back on and set the bottle on the table. Then she turned to face the man whose voice she knew so well. 'Thank you.' Inexplicably, she felt a lump in the back of her throat as she took the long-stemmed hot-house roses he held out to her.

'Your namesake. I thought they were appropriate.'

They were yellow, Rose noted, not red, the traditional gift expressing love. She had no idea what to read into that.

They looked at each other wordlessly for several seconds.

No one seemed to notice. How odd that now he had met someone else Jack had developed a romantic streak. Or maybe I quashed it, she admitted honestly, recalling times he had bought her gifts. Maybe Laura was right about Jack all along. Her view was that having lost David in such a tragic manner she was terrified of giving or receiving love again in case the same thing happened twice. But it was too late now. Rose had shut him out. Whatever might have been possible between her and Jack was no longer viable with Anna on the scene. The tears which had threatened did not fall. But where was Anna? There were no strange faces, nothing in the kitchen had changed, except the level of conversation was a little noisier.

'Anna couldn't make it, she sends her apologies,' Jack said, reading her mind. 'May I?' He picked up a whisky bottle.

'Of course.' Tall, dark and handsome, Rose thought as she watched him pour his drink with strong hands. It ought to have been a cliché, she thought, but in Jack's case it wasn't. She could smell his clean, masculine smell and felt a desire to touch him. 'She's not ill, is she?'

'No.' A flicker of a smile crossed his face. It was typical of Rose, she just had to know. He would bet she had been longing to meet Anna. But Jack hadn't spoken to her, they had agreed to wait until after Christmas, by which time Jack should have come to a decision. To his surprise Anna had already told him she had other plans, that she was going to a friend's house. There would be three of them, three women, all now single, who planned to spoil themselves for a change instead of catering to men and families. Jack had been surprised but not particularly bothered. To him each day was much the same as the next. It had been different when his boys were small.

'Come and say hello to my parents.' Rose almost took his hand, but didn't. Her mood had lifted. Jack was there and he'd come alone. 'Dad's the DJ but it'll be mostly jazz and I know you like it.'

They moved through the throng of the people Rose knew. Geoff Carter, the gallery owner, was deep in conversation with Maddy Duke, Rose's friend from St Ives. She was, as usual, dressed in a bizarre assortment of clothes and the tangle of mousy-blonde hair which hung down her back was adorned with tiny glittering clips. She ran a gift shop and produced much of the craft herself.

Rose looked around and felt almost superfluous at her own party, but maybe that was the way a good hostess should feel. There was no need to introduce people, they either already knew one another or had been introduced by someone else.

Trevor looked flushed. He'd probably had a few drinks before he arrived. Rose hoped it wouldn't lead to another row between him and Laura, but then, Laura wasn't stinting herself in the kitchen either.

'Jack, lovely to see you.' Evelyn reached up to kiss his cheek.

Arthur extended his hand. 'Hello, Jack. Benny Goodman. One of my favourites.' He nodded towards the CD player in the corner.

'One of mine, too,' Jack said, aware that Evelyn was trying to peer around him.

'Is your, uh, young lady here?'

'No. She couldn't make it.' Jack bit his lip. Like mother, like daughter. Evelyn, too, wanted to know why not but he wouldn't satisfy their curiosity. Couldn't, in fact, he realised, because he had no idea where he stood with Anna. And yet, deep down, he was glad he had come on his own. It would have been hard for Anna, meeting a whole new group of people, many of whom Jack had known for most of his life. But was that the only reason he felt glad? He would think about it later.

Someone slapped him on the shoulder. 'Good to see you.'

Jack turned around. Rose had disappeared. 'Hi, Barry, quite a do, isn't it?' He nodded at the assembled group comprising Doreen Clarke and her husband, Maddy Duke and Geoff Carter and the other various people that Rose had collected along the way. They all liked her, and she them, and for such a disparate group that said a lot about her.

'Rose knows how to entertain.'

Jack nodded. It was true, but Barry was always so defensive of her. Barry would certainly know about Anna. Surely he didn't disapprove, not if it left the coast clear for him.

'Did you come on your own?'

It was obvious he had but in true Cornish fashion the question had to be asked. 'Yes, I did.'

Barry pushed his glasses into place. It made no difference. Rose would never love him in any way other than as a friend. For years he had had to content himself with that

209

knowledge. 'Can I get you another drink?'

'Good idea.'

Rose was in the kitchen dispensing serviettes, plates and cutlery. 'Barry, would you tell everyone they can come and help themselves?' she asked.

It was only when people were doing so that Jack had a chance to speak to Rose properly. They were at one side of the kitchen, near the door. 'I wondered if Joel would be here. You said his parents would be away and I know you, every lame duck, etc.'

Rose grinned. She was flushed and a little flustered but Jack knew this was from the effort of ensuring her guests were all right. 'He's staying with a friend and his family. Besides, it's hardly his sort of thing. Look, Jack, I know this isn't really the time or place but Louisa came to see me. No, don't say it.' She extended a warning hand. 'I didn't invite her. That family seems to have a penchant for turning up on my doorstep unannounced. Anyway, she never got to the point of her visit. All she really told me was how much she loved her husband, or maybe that's just what she wanted me to hear.'

'Rogues have a certain charm for some women, and they often command more loyalty than they deserve.'

'Yes. Quite.'

Jack raised an eyebrow, unsure what the enigmatic remark meant.

Rose studied him, unsure whether she ought to go on. He leant, one arm against the door frame, looking down at her. He was casually dressed in tan trousers and a yellow shirt unbuttoned at the neck. He had discarded his brown flecked jacket because of the heat generated by such a big crowd. 'Anyway, there was a letter in her bag with a foreign stamp.'

'Rose, you didn't . . . ?'

'Of course not. What on earth do you take me for? The bag was open beside her.' She turned to hand Cyril Clarke a plate. 'Dig in,' she told him. 'I don't want anything left over.'

'I will, maid. 'Tis a lovely spread.'

Rose and Jack were silent, watching with admiration as Cyril filled his plate to overflowing and carried it to a corner of the kitchen where he ate, standing up and without spilling anything.

'Aren't you eating, Rose?' Laura's hand hovered over a plate. Trevor stood beside her filling his with whatever was within his reach.

'Later, when everyone's helped themselves.'

'What about you, Jack?'

'Later.' He wondered why she was looking at him in such a peculiar manner. Her expression was almost a leer. He had known her since childhood; she had only ever treated him like a brother. 'Okay,' he said, turning to face Rose. 'Tell me about this letter.'

Rose shrugged. 'I'm not sure there is anything to tell. But because Louisa showed no signs of concern when Frank disappeared I wondered, maybe, if she knew where he was all along.'

'Come off it, you thought he was dead, that he'd been transported to the mists of Bodmin Moor in a deep freeze.'

Put like that it sounded ridiculous. Rose blushed. Jack

frequently made her feel uncomfortable. 'Yes, well, that was then.'

'And now?'

'Now I think he's abroad. I think he took off in his boat. I think Louisa might know exactly where he is.'

'Then why isn't she with him? Why not go too, especially if, as she claims, she loves him so much?'

'Because they couldn't both disappear at the same time, not if some crime has been committed.'

Rose had a point, but as far as the police were concerned Frank Jordan was not wanted in connection with any crime. But nothing seemed to explain Wendy's presence at the farmhouse or Miranda's decision to disappear then reappear at a time when solicitors were seeking her father. Like Rose, he suspected her reasons for leaving in the first place went far deeper than any she had ever admitted to. 'When Miranda came here that first time, what did she want to talk to you about?'

'About Joel, about arranging to meet him.'

'Nothing else?'

'No. The only other thing she said was that she was too embarrassed to face her aunt and uncle.'

'It's a shame they're away I'd have liked to have spoken to them. And the second time, when she came with Joel. What did she talk about then, apart from the boat, I mean?'

'It's odd. They came as a sort of deputation, as if they had some hard facts but then decided against telling me what they were. Miranda hedged. She said she believed something bad may have happened to her father and then, with a throw-away line, she said she had suspected her mother of having something to do with it but now she knew better.'

Jack nodded and went across to the table to refill their glasses. The kitchen was a little less crowded now and the noise level had dropped as people were eating. He poured white wine for Rose although it was no longer chilled. Handing her her glass he asked, 'Rose why would a near stranger like Miranda come to you to confide such a thing?'

'I've no idea. People do sometimes.'

Indeed they do, Jack thought. But this time he believed Rose to be wrong, that no matter how deep they dug, there would be little to be found. The overseas letter probably had an innocent explanation; a distant cousin, a pen-friend, an old school mate.

'But why say it at all? Why bring her mother into it if she thinks she's innocent? I believe Miranda knows something is wrong but she isn't sure what. I think she was looking to me, as an outsider, to help her. I think she finally came to realise that she couldn't hide from whatever ghosts were haunting her and she came back to face them.'

'You seem to have been doing an awful lot of thinking, Rose. Now I'll tell you what I think. I think you won't be satisfied until, well, to coin a phrase, until you know the ins and outs of the cat's backside.'

'In that case I think I'll circulate,' she said with a toss of her head. Bugger him, she thought as she flounced off, I just wish he'd take this seriously.

In the sitting room she handed out the presents she had bought for Laura, Trevor, Barry and Maddy and received some of her own in return. She placed them beneath the tree. Jack had brought flowers, she had nothing to give him in return but, at that moment, she was glad.

The party went on longer than she had anticipated. At eleven-thirty Rose and Evelyn stood in the kitchen surveying the wreckage. Litter covered every surface. Rose had insisted that Doreen and Cyril and Barry Rowe took some of the left-over food home with them.

'Let's get stuck in,' Evelyn said, slipping on Rose's apron before taking a pair of rubber gloves from beneath the sink. She began on the glasses whilst Rose filled a bin-liner with paper plates and half-eaten food. Arthur was busy tidying the sitting room.

'Amazing,' he said when he finally joined them, a glass of malt whisky in his hand. 'No cigarette burns, no mess on the carpet. What civilised friends you have.'

'Not all of them,' Rose muttered as she carried the plastic bag outside to the bin. Jack, she recalled, had left without bothering to say goodnight.

CHAPTER FIFTEEN

Michael was surprised to feel nervous as he approached the farmhouse. He supposed the all-female household would be watching him closely. However, Miranda greeted him warmly, throwing her arms around him as soon as she opened the door, and her mother and aunt seemed friendly, if not effusive in their welcome. It would be a quiet Christmas but that didn't matter as long as he was with Miranda.

'Let me show you your room,' she said as soon as he stepped into the hallway 'Then I'll explain the peculiarities of the house. It's fun, actually, a bit like living in a previous era.'

Once he had been taken all around the house and told how things worked, he wondered why the two women had chosen to live as they did. Keeping the fires going and the lamps trimmed or whatever they did to them must be time-consuming.

In the kitchen he turned to Miranda, placed a finger under her chin and tilted her head towards him. 'I love you,' he said simply. 'I only realised how much once you had left. Have you missed me at all?'

Miranda nodded, head down now, the ringlets of hair falling forward and hiding the feelings she knew would be reflected in her face. 'Michael, I've had a long chat with my mother. I've decided I want to go to university after all.' She looked up and grinned. 'But that doesn't mean I don't love you.'

'No problem then.' Michael grinned back. It was what he had wanted to hear. 'No matter where you go we can still see each other most weekends.'

'Yes, we can. Come on, let's go through. They'll be gasping for a sherry or something and they won't start without us. Hopefully we can induce some Christmas cheer into my Aunt Wendy. I don't know what's the matter with her lately.' Miranda had matured enough to know that although she loved Michael now things might be very different once she started studying again. They would both meet other people, possibly fall in love with one of them, but for the moment she was happy. For the moment there was Christmas to get through then she would consider having another talk with Rose Trevelyan. Something was wrong, Miranda knew that. Even her mother was being cagey. Mrs Trevelyan, she was certain, would get to the bottom of whatever mystery her family had created. And when Uncle Roger and Petra returned she would face them, too. It was time things were out in the open.

It soon became obvious that Louisa liked Michael, and even Wendy's stiff attitude softened a little in the presence of the young man. No one mentioned Frank Jordan. Michael was curious; all he knew was that the man had walked out on his family about the same time as Miranda arrived in

216

London. He had thought Christmas might have brought her father to mind.

They ate lots of good food, took long walks and returned to the blazing fire tired and content to play Scrabble or cards or simply to talk. Despite the quiet way in which they spent their time, the three days passed quickly.

'I can't believe I enjoyed it so much,' Michael said on the day he left. He had promised to spend the New Year with his own family.

Miranda laughed. He had not meant to be rude, he was used to the ways of the city, to noise and parties and pubs. She knew what he meant and had expected him to be bored. She waved as he drove away, knowing that she would miss him.

A low-lying mist covered the moor lending it a strange, eerie quality. The branches of the few stunted trees rose through it, appearing to have no trunks. She shivered, a little lost now that Michael had gone, and wondered when she would see him again and how she would occupy herself until October.

Shutting the door she went back inside. Halfway up the stairs on her way to her room her mother called out. 'Miranda, would you bring down my reading glasses, please? I think I left them beside my bed.'

She'd wanted some time alone, to assess the changes that acknowledging her feelings would bring to her life, but first she would fetch the glasses.

She saw the leather case on the bedside cabinet and picked it up. The drawer wasn't properly closed. Naturally tidy, Miranda put out a hand to push it to. Her fingers froze on the knob. No, she thought, it can't be true.

Unable to help herself she pulled the drawer open and took a closer look. She knew then for certain that she had had every reason to be suspicious.

Christmas and Boxing Day were fairly quiet for Rose and her parents, too. They had a couple of drinks with Laura and Trevor and their family then returned to Rose's house for a late Christmas lunch. Too much food had been counteracted by long walks. On the 26th Barry had driven them up to Newquay where they'd watched the famous surf rolling up over the golden sands of Fistral Bay. Even in the sharp, clean wind there were a few surfers, protected by wetsuits, enjoying the near-perfect conditions. In the summer the place was packed.

They walked around the headland, the wind whipping at their clothes. Arthur was sporting his new trilby with which he was delighted. Evelyn had grinned when he had dumped the old one in Rose's bin with great ceremony. Evelyn, also thrilled, had changed into her silver-threaded cardigan on Christmas Day as soon as she'd opened the gift-wrapped package.

The sky was an even blue; the sea, a shade darker, was crested with white. Gulls wheeled overhead and the occasional jackdaw squawked at them as they passed. Each side of them was the rough grass which survived the gales and the salt-laden air. Rose itched to paint the scenery around her, but the colours were so startlingly clear no one not witnessing that same scene would believe they were true.

They drove back through the town, mainly shut up

for the winter, and headed back to Newlyn.

'Are you coming in for a cup of tea?' Rose asked, when Barry delivered them to the door.

'No. I've got a few things to do.' He kissed her cheek and reversed back down the drive, not wishing to outstay his welcome. Rose needed some time alone with her parents.

'I feel completely invigorated,' Evelyn said, sinking into an armchair. 'All that fresh air, it was wonderful.'

'Well, just stay there and I'll fill the kettle.' Rose did so, realising that for the past two days she had thought of nothing but providing food and pleasure for her guests. Barry had stayed until seven on Christmas night and then left them to it. He had turned up again at ten that morning to take them out for the day. Having eaten a proper breakfast with grilled slices of Cornish hog's pudding, they had decided to forego lunch, no one had been hungry.

Tomorrow her parents were leaving. Rose would miss them but she was also looking forward to getting back to work. If the weather remained as it was her plans for Bodmin Moor could go ahead. Already she saw the scene in her mind although she hadn't actually found a location. That was part of the enjoyment, driving or walking until she came to an ideal spot.

They spent the last evening at home, winding down from the festivities.

'Have you any plans for New Year's Eve?' Arthur asked before they went to bed.

'I'm going to Laura's. It isn't a party, there'll just be a few of us. Her family will have gone and we've usually sated ourselves by then.'

'Is Barry going with you?'

'He'll be there, Laura always invites him.'

Arthur nodded. The subject of Jack had been taboo since the night he had left without saying goodbye. He wondered if Rose was more to blame than Jack, if she had upset him in some way. It wouldn't surprise him.

'I don't believe it after yesterday,' Rose said the following morning when they assembled in the kitchen for breakfast. 'Typical West Penwith weather.'

The rain was sheeting down, hitting the roof of the shed and bouncing back up again. Rivulets of water ran down the drive and snaked down the window. 'It won't be much fun driving back in this. Why don't you stay another night?'

Evelyn looked at Arthur. 'What do you think?'

'We're supposed to be going to the Hutchinsons' for lunch tomorrow, and it might still be raining anyway.'

'You're right. Thank you, Rose, but I think we'll stick to our plans.'

Rose smiled. They were tired and wanted to get home. Her father was a good driver and a sensible man, he would not take risks in such weather. Rose was also tired, how much more so must they be? There had been the party and Christmas Day and a long day out in Newquay, and they had, over the four days, walked miles. She understood and did not press them.

They ate fruit and yoghurt and emptied the coffee machine between them. 'If you're all packed, shall we make a move?' Arthur suggested.

'Yes. I'm ready.'

He went upstairs to bring down their bag, now

overflowing with the presents they had received. Rose had bought small gifts as well as the main ones. Their gifts to her had been vouchers for theatre tickets which she could use at the Theatre Royal in Plymouth, or any other city, a bottle of her favourite perfume and a beautiful lacy nightdress.

Tears filled Rose's eyes as they pulled away, but the rain, blowing into her face, disguised the ones which fell. She hated partings, especially from her parents, but she knew by the evening she would be back in her old routine and glad for it.

She spent the rest of the day cleaning the kitchen and sorting out the leftover food and the deep freeze. With a glass of wine in her hand she got out a large-scale map and studied it. The rain had abated but the sky was still grey. The forecast for tomorrow was good but that didn't mean anything. In that part of the world it was far too changeable to be predictable.

'Damn.' The ringing telephone made her jump. 'Hello?'

'Mrs Trevelyan, it's Miranda. Can I come and see you tomorrow?'

Her voice was no more than a whisper, she obviously did not want the conversation to be overheard. Again? Rose thought. 'Yes,' she heard herself saying, wondering how she had forgotten the family so easily 'Can you make it in the morning?'

'Yes, I'll leave here as early as I can.'

'I'll see you when you get here, then.' Rose hung up. So it was all going to start again. The Penhaligons would be back in a couple of days; hopefully she could hand the whole mess over to them. Jack had not been in touch since the party so he couldn't help. Rose was certain that she was now out of his life altogether.

I'll have an early night, she decided, get Miranda out of the way in the morning, then I'm definitely going to do some work.

Jack picked up the telephone and dialled Anna's number. She answered almost immediately as if she had been standing by the phone waiting for his call. 'Did you have a good Christmas?' she asked almost shyly.

'Yes, thanks. Did you?'

'We had a great time.'

What do I say now? Jack thought. He had spent the morning of the twenty-fifth mooching about the house waiting for the Mount's Bay Inn to open for its traditional two hours. It was the same small pub on the seafront which Rose often frequented. She was not there that day. When the pub closed he went back to his flat, cooked a meal and watched television. He was not lonely, he never was. He liked his own company. Nor was he miserable or full of self-pity. People made such a fuss about spending Christmas together and mostly regretted it after a few days. But he was not about to tell Anna how he had spent his time.

'How did the party go?' she asked in order to break the silence.

'Very well. Look, Anna, I've had a chance to think things over. I want to see you, you know that, but Rose is my friend, I can't just abandon her.'

'I see.'

'Meaning what?'

'Meaning, Jack, that I can never be sure of you.'

'That's unreasonable, Anna, and you know it. We're not exactly teenagers, adults can have friendships outside of relationships without it meaning something more.'

Anna sighed. 'I know that. I didn't mean to sound childish, really I didn't. It's just that – oh, damn it. You're a good, decent man, Jack, and maybe that's why you can't hide your feelings. What you feel for Rose is more than friendship. I can hear it in your voice every time you say her name.'

She's right, Jack thought, but what do I do about it? 'So where does that leave us?'

'As friends. We can have the odd drink, or a meal. No hard feelings, honestly. I needed to know, you see, before – well, it doesn't matter.'

It did matter. Jack knew from her last words that Anna felt more for him than he had realised and had acted this way in order to prevent herself from being hurt. 'Friends, then,' he said, unsure if disappointment or relief was in the ascendancy.

'I'll see you, Jack. Goodbye.'

Anna had replaced the receiver before he could say anything more. He stood by the phone staring at it as if it had all the answers. He suddenly realised that what he wanted most in the world was to see Rose.

He glanced out of the window. It was a grey day but at least it wasn't raining. Too grey for Rose to be working, he hoped. He pulled on a jacket and strode down Morrab Road to the Queen's Hotel where he crossed over to the Promenade and began to walk swiftly towards Newlyn.

By the time he had reached her drive he was breathless. He swore. A car was parked behind hers. A car which he recognised. But it was too late. Rose and Miranda were in the kitchen and they had seen him. He could not decipher Rose's expression as she opened the door to him, but it was not particularly welcoming. 'Sorry, I thought with your parents gone you'd be alone. Hello, Miranda.'

'Hello.'

'Coffee?' Rose walked towards the worktop and took a mug from its tree.

Jack sat down. There was an air of tension in the room. He wondered what they had been talking about. Maybe it was fortunate he had arrived, Rose often managed to find herself in trouble she couldn't handle.

'Miranda was on her way over to see Joel and called in here first,' Rose began.

'We have to tell him, Rose,' Miranda interrupted. 'I can't go on like this, not knowing, not being able to trust my family.'

'Tell me what?' Jack looked from one to the other.

'You tell him, Rose.'

Rose placed Jack's coffee on the table and sat down. Her hands were in her lap. 'Miranda found some letters addressed to her mother. The postmarks were recent. They were from Spain. Miranda is convinced it's her father's handwriting. So far, I, and now you, are the only people to know this, apart from Louisa, obviously.'

Steam spiralled up from Jack's coffee. He took a sip and burnt his mouth. Was one of those letters the one Rose had seen? And if so, what was going on? Even if Louisa had known all along where her husband was, it didn't mean anything illegal had taken place.

'Inspector Pearce, I know my father owed money to Uncle Roger. Do you think that's why he disappeared?'

'Did he tell you this?'

'No. Joel did.'

'Have you any idea of the figure?'

Miranda looked at the floor. Her face was flushed. 'Somewhere around two hundred thousand pounds. Joel overheard his parents discussing what to do about it. They're rich, Uncle Roger makes loads of money but even so that's an awful lot of money and a debt's a debt.'

Yes, that amount was worth disappearing for. And if Frank Jordan owed one person he might also owe others. 'Where are the letters?'

'At home. In my mother's bedroom drawer.'

There was absolutely no chance of obtaining a search warrant. Jack knew something ought to be done, but he wasn't sure what. 'When do the Penhaligons get back?' he asked.

'The day after tomorrow.'

He would speak to them. It was the least he could do. If Jordan was in Spain he had either reapplied for a passport or managed to obtain a false one.

'Was there something in particular you wanted?' Rose asked, suddenly realising he had given no reason for his unexpected visit.

'Yes. I could have rung, but I fancied a walk. I came to invite you out for a meal.' It was far easier to ask in the company of a third party. He did not have to offer any

225

explanations in front of Miranda and he knew Rose would ask for none.

'When?'

'How about tonight?'

Rose was aware of the girl watching them and tried to remain cool and in control, but inwardly she was pleased, more than pleased. She hoped she wasn't blushing. How could it be that it was only yesterday her parents had left and she had felt so low? 'Yes, tonight's fine.'

'Good.'

'Can you do anything? About the letters, I mean?' she added quickly aware of Jack's almost casual response to her answer. He, too, was more pleased than he was trying to pretend.

'Not until I've spoken to Miranda's uncle. Look . . .' he turned to the girl. 'Are you sure she doesn't have relatives or a penfriend in Spain?'

'No relatives, no. And she's never mentioned a pen-friend.'

'Then don't say a word about this to anyone. I'm sure there'll be an innocent explanation, but for now it's best not to let your mother know what you've told me.'

Miranda nodded as she stood. 'I'll go and see Joel now, he's expecting me.' She paused. 'My aunt and uncle will be back soon. I intend to see them. I owe them an apology and an explanation.'

'Don't even mention this conversation to Joel,' Jack added firmly.

'Okay.'

Rose saw her to the door. Now she was alone with Jack she felt awkward. 'What time tonight?' she asked.

'Sevenish?'

'I'll meet you in the Yacht, shall I?'

'I'll be there.'

Jack stood, ready to leave. It was obvious he didn't want to talk further just then. If he had something to tell her no doubt he would do so later. Rose shook her head as she watched him go. She still had no idea where she stood with him. He might even decide not to turn up later. It didn't matter, she knew most of the early evening customers in the Yacht. It was an art deco pub, set back from the seafront opposite the open-air swimming pool which had also been built in the thirties. I'll doll myself up, she thought as she picked up the canvas bag which contained her painting equipment. I'll make a real effort for once.

Echoing her own upswing in mood, the weather changed. The sky began to clear, greyness gave way to white cloud interspersed with ever-increasing patches of blue. Outside the air smelt of damp foliage and earth, a clean refreshing smell. Rose felt good. It was only ten-thirty. She would drive to the moors and do some work.

CHAPTER SIXTEEN

Petra and Roger were glad to be home. Although their return flight had been delayed, somewhat spoiling the last few hours, the break had relaxed them and they were ready to face a new year.

Joel had heard the car and went to open the door. 'Hi,' he said, smiling broadly. 'Welcome home.' It was the first time he had been left on his own and he had been surprised by how much he had missed his parents even though he tended to take them for granted when they were around. And with all that had been going on he was looking forward to what he had come to recognise as his father's sound way of thinking. That, of course, was down to Rose Trevelyan. He respected her, as a woman as well as an artist. If he could ever be half as talented he would be extremely happy. Joel's future was now set, as was Miranda's. He was pleased for her but slightly jealous of her relationship with Michael, a man he had not met. It was a sibling jealousy rather than a sexual one.

'It's great to be home,' Roger said as he patted his son on the shoulder.

Petra glanced around anxiously as she entered the lounge, then she smiled. 'No wild parties, then?' The house was tidy but the furniture could do with a polish. The cleaner had been given two weeks' holiday.

'Far from it.' He paused. 'Mum, Miranda's been here.'

'Miranda?' Her face paled beneath the light tan she had acquired in Madeira.

'Yes.'

'How is she?' Petra wasn't sure what else to say.

'She's fine. She looks well, but I don't think she's very happy.'

Petra sat down. 'Why did she go away, Joel? Did she tell you?'

'I'm not sure. Oh, hell, I suppose you ought to know. I think the police might want to talk to you.'

'The police?' Roger stood in the doorway, his car coat over his arm. 'I've put the cases upstairs, love. What's this about the police?' he asked, turning back to Joel. 'It was time they took some notice. They haven't found Frank, have they?'

'No, but I think they're finally taking you seriously, about Uncle Frank, that is. You see, Dad, I was just telling Mum, Miranda's been here.'

'Knowing we were away, I take it. I don't understand any of this, only that my brother-in-law owes me money which I'm never likely to see again.

'Anyway, what's up with the girl? Why can't she come out in the open, doesn't she realise she's had us worried sick?'

Joel took a deep breath. 'We've been to Uncle Frank's

lock-up. The boat wasn't there but his holdall was, with his clothes and passport and stuff. The police took it away.'

'My God, what on earth's been going on in our absence? I think I need a drink.' He turned to where the bottles were kept and poured a stiff whisky. Without asking Petra he poured her one, too. Then he lit a cigar which filled the room with its not unpleasant odour. 'I think you'd better start at the beginning, son. I want to know everything that's happened since we've been away.' He stood in front of the fire which Joel had thoughtfully lit knowing that his parents would feel the difference in temperature. It crackled cheerfully in the grate.

It took Joel almost twenty minutes to explain and even then there were no hard facts to impart, only supposition.

'Louisa killed Frank? That's ridiculous.'

'I know, but that's what we all thought at first. Then it seemed more likely that Wendy might have done.'

'The "we" includes Rose Trevelyan, no doubt.' Roger's smile was wry. He had summed up Rose as quickly as she had done him. Asking her to keep her ear to the ground, he had noticed the expression on her face and he realised she was the sort of woman who would go to further lengths than that.

'Yes. But now there's a new development.'

'Which is?'

'Miranda told me there are some letters. She saw them in a drawer, she's certain they were from her father. From Spain.' Joel blushed. Inspector Pearce had told Miranda to keep this information to herself but they had always shared things. He hoped he hadn't got her into trouble.

'So that's where he's hiding.' Roger turned to flick ash into the fireplace.

'But Roger, don't you see what this means? Louisa's known all along where he was but Miranda didn't. How could she do that to the girl. All right, Miranda and Frank weren't close but he was still her father.'

'It's beyond me, Petra, but if the police are finally doing something about it perhaps we'll eventually find out what the bloody family are playing at. And perhaps I'll get my money back. It's Frank's debt, not Louisa's, whatever she might have done I couldn't ask her for it.' He reached for his glass which he had placed on the mantelpiece and went to refill it. 'I think I'll give Rose Trevelyan a ring. I'd like to find out what she knows before we speak to the police.'

But Rose was either out or not answering the telephone. He left a message for her to ring back then uncharacteristically offered to help his wife to unpack.

Rose leant against the sink in Laura's neat but cramped kitchen. She and Trevor had lived there all of their married life and had no intention of moving. They had brought up three sons there and, to them, the place now seemed spacious. Rose was amazed how they coped when their now extended family came to stay, although neighbours always helped out with the use of a spare room. That was the beauty of such a small community, people were always willing to help.

'So,' Laura said, tossing back her hair as steam rose as she added something to the pan on the stove. 'What sort of trouble are you in this time?'

231

'I'm not in trouble, Laura, just helping some new friends. They're young and confused and, I think, just a bit frightened.'

Laura snorted and looked over her thin shoulder. 'You've only known them for a few weeks. I don't know how you do it.' She grinned. 'Our glasses are empty, it's unlike you to be so dilatory. Hurry up, it's ready.'

They sat at the table to eat beef in red wine, accompanied by fresh vegetables. Like Rose, Laura believed in eating well, and local fresh food was better quality than any that could be purchased in a supermarket.

'There's some scam going on,' Rose said, unable to think of anything but Frank Jordan. 'But I just can't make out what it is. It seems he's alive and living in Spain, if what Miranda tells me is right, and I did see one of those letters myself. And there's all the paintings and antiques.'

'What paintings?' Laura speared some broccoli.

'Louisa's house is full of them. They've got to be worth a fortune.'

'But you said they live without electricity and everything.'

'I know. Still, given the choice, I'd rather have the paintings.'

'That's because you're an artist. I know what I'd prefer. Can't you talk about anything else?' She leant forward. 'Anyway, I want to know how it went with Jack on Saturday.'

Rose blushed. 'I'm not sure. He refuses to talk about Anna.'

'Hmm. I wonder if she exists.'

'What're you talking about? Jack wouldn't lie to me.'

'Ah, listen to you. You're suddenly very defensive of him. Well, she didn't come to your party either, did she?'

'Don't grin at me like a bloody Cheshire cat.'

'Teasy tonight, aren't we?'

Rose laughed. Laura always knew how to put her in her place.

'Come on, we were talking about Jack.'

'All right. We met in the Yacht and had a couple of drinks then we walked back across the Promenade and had a meal in the Newlyn Laundry restaurant. He'd already booked it.' Rose bit her lip. She hadn't forgotten it was where Jack had taken Anna; neither had Laura.

'Which meant he knew you'd accept his invitation.'

'Or Anna had let him down.'

'How cynical you've become, my dear. Of course Anna didn't let him down, if anything it would've been the other way around. It's you Jack wants, that's obvious to everyone except you.'

Rose shook her head. It had been an enjoyable evening although their old intimacy had been missing. They had talked of general things; not Anna, not the Penhaligons, not the sisters. Rose still didn't know what footing their relationship was on. And I didn't have the courage to ask, she admitted. But she had invited him for a meal in a week's time, an invitation he had accepted very quickly. He hadn't said he needed to check with Anna, or he'd let her know. Just, 'I'd love that. Thank you.' Then he had paid the bill and walked her home.

Laura raised her eyebrows. 'And?' she asked when Rose had finished speaking.

'And nothing. He went home himself then.' It was time to change the subject.

They chatted until gone eleven when Trevor returned from a card game and Rose decided it was time to leave.

There was one message for her but it was too late to return Roger Penhaligon's call. She would do so first thing in the morning.

'Rose, hello. Did you have a good Christmas? Joel told me what a feast you put on for him and Miranda.'

So he knows all about it, Rose thought. 'Yes. And you? Good holiday?'

'One of the best. Now look, Inspector Pearce just called. He's coming over to see us this morning. Could I ask you a favour? We'd like it if you were here, too.'

I'll see Jack again, she thought, wondering why that was more important than what she might learn. 'Yes. What time?'

'Come as soon as you're ready. We can have a chat first. Oh, by the way, Miranda will be here, Joel rang her earlier. I thought it was for the best if he sees us all together so we can all put in our twopence worth.'

'That's fine.' Rose glanced at her watch. 'I'll leave here in about half an hour.' She hung up. Once again work would have to wait, but the sooner this was all over with the sooner she could settle down again. Well, maybe in a few days' time. It's New Year's Eve, she thought. I'd completely forgotten. Tonight she would be at Laura's again. There were only going to be eight of them. Four couples, not that she and Barry were a couple. And then, hopefully, she could get back into her usual routine. And Jack, how would he be celebrating? It was best not to think about it.

Within twenty-five minutes she was on her way. The

weather was almost springlike. Wisps of cloud floated across the sky occasionally obscuring the pale sun and causing shadows to dance across the countryside which became more barren with each passing mile. There was very little traffic on the St Just road. She turned into the Penhaligons' gateway and parked.

Petra opened the door to her and smiled. 'We're all here, except Inspector Pearce. He'd said he'd come at about ten-thirty. Come on in.'

Rose followed her into the lovely lounge and said hello to those present. Both Miranda and Joel sat on the edge of their seats as if they were guilty of something. Perhaps they were.

For twenty minutes they discussed all they knew then, when the doorbell rang, Roger went to let Jack in and Petra went to get the coffee.

'I didn't expect to see you here, Rose,' Jack said when Roger showed him in.

'I was invited,' she replied defensively. 'Does it matter?'

'Of course not.' He smiled to soften the harshness of his tone. He had been unprepared to see her and hoped it wouldn't affect his professionalism. 'Firstly,' he began, once he was seated and had established how much the Penhaligons knew, 'even if these letters exist, there is no way I can ask to see them.'

'They do exist,' Miranda stated firmly.

'Yes, they do,' Rose added

'Okay. But what we can do is to make some inquiries in Spain. The boat for a start, that should be traceable, if it hasn't already been sold.'

Roger shook his head. He was in the process of lighting

up. He leant back to put his lighter in his jacket pocket and blew a stream of smoke at the ceiling. 'He loved that boat, I can't believe he'd have sold it.'

'If we find the boat, we might find him. Mr Penhaligon, may I ask you a very personal question?'

'Feel free.'

'Did Frank Jordan owe you money?'

'Ah, that. There are no secrets down here, are there, Inspector Pearce? Yes, he did. Is that why he disappeared? He knew there was no rush to pay me back, I made that clear from the start. It was an interest-free loan, too.'

'That was very generous.'

'Don't sound so cynical. I did it for Louisa, my sister. She'd bailed him out before, I didn't want to see her suffer any further financial loss. And, without meaning to sound boastful, we can afford it.'

'I see. Miranda, what made you so sure something had happened to your father?'

'I don't really know.' Her face was pale and she looked as if she hadn't had much sleep. 'He just left, without saying anything, and Mum didn't seem to care. She loved him, idolised him, almost. Even I could see that. Then all of a sudden she was acting as if he had never existed. She even refused to talk about it. I thought . . . well, never mind. I just felt I needed to get away.'

'Jack, I don't know if this is relevant, but it seems only Wendy was aware he was leaving. She was the only one there at the time,' Rose told him.

Although Jack already knew that, he asked, 'Who told you this?'

'Miranda did.'

'And who told you, Miranda?'

'My mother.'

The same source I heard it from. Then it might not be true, he thought. Mrs Louisa Jordan was conveniently out of the house all morning on the day before they moved. Sorting out final details, she had claimed, yet surely they would have been attended to before then? 'Right, let's go over everything once more then I'll get on to the Spanish authorities.' Jack was now convinced that Rose was right, that something was wrong, but he didn't know what. Louisa's behaviour was hard to fathom.

An hour later he left. Driving back to Camborne he realised that he understood Miranda a little better. Immaturity had caused her to panic and she had run away from a situation which she didn't understand, and probably hadn't wanted to, and which must have frightened her if she believed her mother to be guilty of murder. To a logical mind carrying on as normally as possible would have been the answer but Miranda had been barely eighteen and had had two major upheavals ahead of her: the move and university. My mother would describe her as highly strung, he thought as he pulled into the police station car park.

He would do as he had promised and see if Frank Jordan could be located in Spain. If he loved his boat as much as people were saying, they might be able to locate the man through it.

'She's spending an awful lot of time in Penzance,' Wendy commented after Miranda had driven away. 'Why do you think that is?'

237

'She's always been fond of Joel, she's missed him.'

'Something's wrong, Louisa. First Frank, then Miranda went missing and you scarcely showed the slightest concern. Why didn't she keep in touch with us? And why all this secrecy now? Is there something you both know that I don't?'

Louisa shook her head. 'The young often have strange ideas. I think she was scared of going to university and didn't want to admit it. The main thing is she's grown up and come back to us.'

They were in the kitchen preparing a few snacks for the evening. There would only be the three of them to see the New Year in. They had severed contact with all their old friends. 'Wendy, there's something I've been meaning to discuss with you.' Louisa continued rolling thin slices of ham around cream cheese. 'I've enjoyed living here, it's been fun in its way, but I've decided to sell the place.'

'What?' Wendy's head jerked up. She dropped the gherkin she had been slicing into circles. 'But we've hardly settled in. Are you sure about this?'

'Yes. I might go abroad, somewhere warm. They say it can be very cheap to live in some Mediterranean countries.'

'I see.' Wendy was rigid with barely controlled anger. 'And where would that leave me?'

'You've got enough money to buy somewhere small, maybe you could go back to Penzance.'

'I gave up everything to be with you; my home, my friends, everything. I've always looked after you. When Frank left, I thought you needed me more than ever. What a fool I must've been.' Her throat burnt and tears filled her eyes. It was a long time since Wendy had cried. 'You've always had everything, looks, money, Frank and a child. You've never really cared for anyone but yourself, have you? You didn't even do anything when Miranda left. Only now can I see how very self-centred you are.'

Louisa whirled around. 'And you're just full of self-pity, which is worse. I didn't ask you to come here and live with me. It was your idea if you recall. And now Miranda's back it's obvious you're jealous of her, too. If you were so concerned why didn't you do anything at the time?'

And suddenly it all surfaced: Wendy's envy of Louisa, Louisa's feeling of superiority over her sister and her unquestionable love for Frank.

'You always wanted Frank, didn't you? Did you think I was blind? You couldn't have him so you tried to poison my feelings for him. He used to laugh at your dismal attempts at flirtation. He loves me, you know. Those other women never mattered to him. And, as for you—'

'How dare you!' Wendy was rigid with fury. It was the first argument they had ever had. Every niggling resentment was suddenly out in the open.

'I've just had the most peculiar telephone call,' Roger Penhaligon said a little while after Rose had left.

'Who from?' Petra was in the kitchen making lunchtime sandwiches.

He explained the content of the conversation briefly. 'Not that it makes much sense, but I get the feeling we'd better do as she asked.'

'I don't like the sound of it. Why has she rung us after all this time?'

'She refused to give any reason. She tried to disguise it, but she sounds in a hell of a state. Shall I take these in?' He gestured towards the plateful of sandwiches.

'Please. We'll have them on our knees. I'll bring in the coffee.'

Roger carried the tray into the lounge where Miranda and Joel were talking quietly. He handed around plates and serviettes and told them to help themselves. When they had done so he said, 'Miranda, why don't you stay the night? We'd love to have you, it'll be like old times. We're having a few friends round, nothing big. What about you, Joel, are you going to that party?'

'I was, but it doesn't matter.' He knew he had never really fitted in with his peer group but it didn't bother him. Far better to be in Miranda's company.

'May I?' Miranda knew her mother and aunt weren't doing anything, and Wendy certainly wouldn't miss her.

She looked both pleased and grateful which added to Roger's suspicions. Something was going on at the house on Bodmin Moor, something she did not want to return to on New Year's Eve of all nights.

'Can I ask, have you forgiven me for not keeping in touch? It was terribly selfish.'

Roger smiled. 'Of course we have.'

'Thank you. It's more than I deserve. I'd better let my mother know where I'll be.'

'There's no need, I'll do it. It's time I spoke to my sister again. Reconciliations all round,' he added. 'Will you give me the number?'

Miranda did so and Roger left the room, ashamed of the

lie he had told and the deceit he had been drawn into, even though from the little he had heard it was for Miranda's sake.

'All settled.' His smile was forced when he returned after ten minutes, the amount of time he had estimated such a call would have taken. 'Now we can catch up on all your news. What do you say, Petra?'

She nodded and continued pouring coffee from the large pot.

Roger went to the cupboard where he kept the drinks and added a measure of brandy to his coffee, aware of his wife's eyes on his back. It was early, even by his standards, but he felt in need of some fortification. It had been a shock seeing Miranda even though he had known she was coming, and then the strange telephone call had come as an even bigger shock. There were far too many things he didn't understand.

With a feeling of dread he tried to concentrate upon what his niece was telling him about her future.

It was very late when Jack got home that night and he was exhausted. The awful news he had to impart could wait until the morning – in fact, he had been requested to leave it until then.

The Spanish police had already come back to them. Jack was still trying to assimilate what they had learnt. Rose had almost been right but not in the way in which she had thought. And now Louisa had been arrested.

Jack was hardly able to think straight. He would have liked Rose to be there. He could have unburdened himself, talked it all over with her. Maybe tomorrow he would do so. He poured a drink and sank into his favourite chair, then he smiled wryly. Imagining eleven thirty was too late to ring her he realised she wouldn't even be at home. In half an hour she would be raising her glass, along with Laura and Barry, to drink to the New Year. At some point during the day he had managed to forget the date.

He didn't hear the church bells ringing at midnight. Before he had finished his drink Jack had fallen asleep in the chair.

CHAPTER SEVENTEEN

Rose opened her eyes and smiled. She didn't feel too bad considering the lateness of the previous night and the amount of wine consumed, she thought as she swung her legs over the side of the bed. Only a hint of a headache and a bit of a thirst, nothing that a glass of water and several mugs of strong coffee wouldn't cure. It had been an enjoyable evening, drinks, good conversation and some of Laura's excellent chilli.

She drew back the curtains and looked out over the bay, which was flooded with sunlight. The bedroom, above the sitting room, enjoyed the same view.

I'll clean the house thoroughly and take down the tree, she decided. Once New Year's Eve was out of the way Rose believed the celebrations were all over and, besides, the tree was beginning to shed its needles. She was not superstitious about leaving it up until Twelfth Night. She would take it outside and saw it up and when she next lit the fire she would burn it. The resin from the pine logs smelt wonderful and they ignited easily. And tomorrow I will paint, she told herself firmly.

Halfway through the morning no trace of Christmas remained. Feeling virtuous and with only the upstairs left to do, Rose rewarded herself with coffee and a cigarette. Later she would have a walk, which she tried to find time for daily then spend the evening doing her hair and her nails. But she had not even sat down when the telephone rang. It was Jack.

'I'd like to talk to you,' he said.

'I told you everything I know yesterday.'

'I know.' He hesitated before continuing, unsure if he was being wise. 'I meant I need to talk to Rose Trevelyan, my friend.'

Rose inhaled sharply She had not expected such seemingly harmless words to induce such a rush of emotion. 'Be my guest.'

'Not over the phone. Can I see you? If you're not busy maybe we could go for a walk. I'm in need of some fresh air.'

Housework was not one of Rose's favourite occupations but she wanted to complete it that day. However, there was something in Jack's voice that told her this was important – and she had intended having a walk later anyway. 'All right. Where shall we meet?'

'I'll pick you up. We can drive somewhere first. It's a lovely day.'

'I'll see you when you get here then.' Rose looked down at her threadbare jeans, the old shirt and the baggy jumper. Too bad, she would have to do.

There would not have been time to change because Jack arrived within ten minutes. He, too, wore jeans, a shirt and a jumper but much neater versions. 'I thought we might go to Lamorna and take the cliff path,' he suggested as Rose pulled on her waxed jacket.

She nodded, pleased now that she would not miss the good weather.

Jack was silent throughout the short journey Rose glanced at his profile. He looked tired and worried. Her stomach churned. She could guess what was coming. He wanted to break the news gently. He was going to move in with Anna or, maybe, even marry her. Could she bear to hear that? He had not mentioned her the other evening. Maybe he feared Rose would create a scene in the restaurant and had waited, maybe that's why he'd chosen an open-air venue today.

Jack parked near the harbour and locked the car. A mild breeze rippled the surface of the milky green water within its walls as they began their ascent over the rough grass.

'I forgot,' Rose said. 'Happy New Year.'

'You, too.' Jack took a deep breath of the crisp, fresh air. 'But it won't be for some.'

Meaning me? Rose wondered. She waited. Jack would get to it in his own time. Her calves had begun to ache before he suggested a rest. They sat on lichen-covered boulders because the grass was still damp and gazed out at the sea.

'You were right and you were wrong,' he began. 'There has been a murder and Louisa Jordan has been charged.'

Rose held her breath and waited.

'Wendy's dead, Rose, not Frank.'

245

'Dead?' Rose was confused. It was Wendy not Anna, Jack wanted to talk to her about.

'Louisa killed her. She claims it was self-defence.'

'My God. Poor Wendy. And poor Miranda.' Rose bowed her head. So Louisa was a murderer after all. 'Jack, I have to ask, was I responsible in any way?' Her voice was low.

'How could you be?' He turned in time to see the misery in her face.

'By interfering.'

'No. It was always on the cards.'

'Can you tell me what happened?'

'You were right about the letters. Frank Jordan has been living in Spain ever since he left Penzance. He took his boat with him. The police traced him easily enough even though he was using false identification. Had he committed a crime out there they might have got on to him sooner. It transpires he not only owes his brother-in-law a small fortune, but there are others as well, others who aren't as patient or tolerant. There was no chance of him ever being able to pay anyone back, nor, it seems, did he have any desire to. He had to get out, and he had the connections to enable him to do so.'

'Are you saying he and Louisa planned it between them?'

'Yes. Everything of any value was put in her name, leaving Jordan just enough to start up in Spain using his new identity. There're enough ex-pats out there for him to con. The idea was that she got away from Penzance and all their old connections then, after a reasonable period, she was to sell everything and join him. She hadn't reckoned on Wendy and didn't know how to handle her. When Frank left she was terrified it would all go wrong, that he'd change his mind about her joining him and she'd be left on her own. At least there would have been Wendy to fall back on. And Wendy knew that.'

'How do you know all this?'

'She admitted it.'

'But why stay in Cornwall?'

'It's her home, Rose. She loves it. She knew she'd have to make a fresh start abroad, but meanwhile she wanted to stay here as long as she could.'

'I can see that, but why the farmhouse? There's no electricity and it's so inconvenient.'

'Because Jordan knew it would appreciate in value. They intended having electricity put in, hence the deep freeze being there. It was almost new but they wouldn't have got much for it if they sold it. Anyway, Louisa realised it would be a waste of their money because the cost of being connected would not add the equivalent value to the price of the house. Besides, several other people had been up against them when it was put up for auction and, despite the lack of amenities, it fetched quite a bit more than the reserve amount. She intended selling the house and the collection of paintings at their now inflated price and going out to Spain.'

'Oh, Jack, I believed Louisa had killed Frank. It's almost as if I've made her murder someone.'

'You mustn't think like that. Look, Miranda had come home. With or without your help she would have gone to see Joel at some point. Even Miranda believed her mother capable of violence.'

'But why did she kill Wendy?'

'There was a tremendous row. Louisa says it was self-defence, that Wendy came for her with a knife in her hand. They struggled and the knife slipped. Her story rings true. It's often the way these things happen.'

'Did you interview her?'

'No. She was taken to Bodmin. I expect someone from Plymouth would have been present. But the details were faxed through to us as we were already involved.'

'Louisa admitted that she had sprung her decision to sell up on Wendy too quickly. She said that, given time, things might have been very different. But she couldn't wait, she couldn't stand being away from Frank any longer. House prices have been increasing rapidly, the time was right, and, unbeknown to her sister, Louisa had already had the paintings and antiques valued and knew what they would fetch at auction.'

'So why didn't she go with Frank in the beginning?'

'Had they both disappeared it might have led people to start looking for them. Of course, they hadn't counted on Miranda's reaction. Anyway, the idea was that people would assume Frank had gone off with someone else and that Louisa had moved to forget her troubles or, maybe, to be out of reach of the people who were looking for Frank. And they needed time for the house and the art collection to increase further in value. But Frank couldn't wait any longer, any more than Louisa could. He wrote, via a post office box number, and asked her to come as soon as possible.'

'So the catalyst was the letter and not Miranda?'

'I think so. You see, despite her feelings for Miranda, it was Frank Louisa loved more than anyone else. He wasn't interested in his daughter but her mother tried hard, tried to convince herself how much Miranda also mattered, but in the end she knew she didn't. Also, once Louisa had seen her again, once she knew she was safe and well with a boyfriend and a career to look forward to, she felt safe in leaving.'

'I think I can see why she wanted that portrait done. If Miranda hadn't come back when she had I'd have completed it and Louisa would have made sure it reached her at some point. It was to be a reminder of the two women who had brought her up.'

Jack nodded. 'You're right, Louisa almost said as much. She admitted her feelings for Miranda were never as strong as they should have been, but has it occurred to you that she also thought the portrait might increase in value, that it might have been meant as a legacy to her daughter?'

It hadn't. Rose was flattered by the idea.

'Louisa was set to go whether or not Miranda returned. Maybe not for a few more months, but certainly within the year.'

'And Frank?'

'He's here now. He loves his wife, you see, he wanted to be by her side. All this talk of other women was just that, a screen they developed between them as part of the plot. He'd never have left her.'

'I wondered about that.' Rose was sceptical, she thought it was more likely to do with the money. 'And his debts?'

'That's something he'll have to sort out. It wouldn't

surprise me if Roger Penhaligon lets him off, he strikes me as a decent sort of man.'

'And Miranda?'

'She took it better than I anticipated. Having lived so long in the belief that her mother was capable of murder it was probably easier for her to accept. By the way she's going to live with the Penhaligons until she goes to university.'

'Will she see her father?'

'That's up to Miranda. At the moment she isn't interested, she can't forgive either of them for their deceit and she still can't understand the almost obsessive bond between them.'

'So Wendy was the only one who really stood in Louisa's way. By making a fuss things had become awkward and that's why she killed her.'

'It's a possibility but I think someone as calculating as Louisa Jordan would have found a way around it if she hadn't stupidly sprung the news so quickly No, I think it was just as she said, it all happened on the spur of the moment.

'Rose, you're shivering. Come on, let's go.'

'I'm not really cold.' But as she stood, hardly able to take it all in, she spotted the rain clouds which had gathered in the west and then noticed the drop in temperature. Jack was right, it was time to go home.

As they made their way back downhill he took her hand. Rose let him. Jack's was large and warm and strong.

It was Rose who was quiet on the journey home. When he pulled up behind her blue Metro Jack turned to her. 'Rose, are you all right?'

'Yes. I've been thinking.'

'Thinking about what?'

'That once we'd have talked this through together, right from the start. We seem to have been on opposite sides lately.'

'Is that how you feel?'

'Yes.' She sighed. 'That, and I feel really tired as well. I think we overdid it at Christmas.'

'Too tired to offer a man a glass of wine?'

She turned to look at him. He was smiling. She smiled back. 'You certainly know how to tempt a woman. It's just what I need. You'd better come in.'

A second glass of wine led to an invitation for Jack to stay to supper.

'Only if you'll allow me to cook it,' he said.

'Carry on,' Rose leant back in her armchair. She was too tired to argue. Last night was catching up on her. And Jack was a better cook than Barry, whose repertoire barely extended beyond pasta. Amidst the clatterings from the kitchen she fell asleep.

A gentle hand on her shoulder woke her. 'It's ready. Come and eat.'

A pungent aroma filled her nostrils. 'Curry?'

'And an excellent one at that, too. There was a plate of turkey in the fridge. I used that. I hope it was all right.'

'That's fine.' Rose had frozen the remains of the eighteen-pound bird she had bought but had taken some out to defrost that morning, believing that at least a week should elapse before even thinking of using up Christmas leftovers.

She relaxed over the meal and felt better for some food. They were talking as they used to talk, discussing all they knew about the Jordans and the Penhaligons, interrupting each other and occasionally laughing. But there was still no mention of Anna.

'Wendy was meant to be alone with Jordan on that last day. Louisa kept out of the way deliberately.' Jack said at one point during the evening. 'He hinted that there was someone else. Every last detail was planned.'

Rose could now believe it. She could almost sympathise with Louisa, who had felt for Frank what she had felt for David. 'I really enjoyed that,' she said, when they had eaten. 'I'll let you cook another time.'

'Will you?'

The way in which he was looking at her made Rose realise just what her words had implied. She didn't know what to say.

'Will you, Rose? You see, the thing is . . . well, Anna and I . . . well, it didn't come to anything in the end.'

'You're not seeing her any more?'

'No. Not since before Christmas.'

Rose bit her lip. It was the first she knew of it and he hadn't said anything at her party. Her face was already flushed from the food, the wine and the warmth of the kitchen. It was now even hotter. It was, she realised, her move, but she didn't have a clue how to make it.

Jack shrugged. 'For some reason it just didn't work out.'

'What didn't? In what way?'

Jack's laugh startled her. 'You never give up, do you? You always have to know every detail.'

'I don't know what you mean.' She fiddled with her knife whilst trying to feign a casual interest. 'What do I always have to know?'

'In this instance, whether or not we made love.'

'Well, did you?' Oh, hell, damn and blast, she thought. She'd had no intention of asking him.

'Almost. Once. But no.'

Relief flooded through her and she felt like cheering, but no way was she going to let Jack Pearce know that. Instead, she sniffed, got to her feet and began to clear the table.

Jack sat back in his chair, arms folded across his chest, and watched her. When Rose finally turned to face him she saw the familiar laughter in his eyes although his firm lips were pressed together.

'You're a bastard, Jack Pearce, do you know that?' she said as she cuffed him with the tea towel.

'Maybe. But remember what we were saying the other week about loveable rogues and how much loyalty they could command?'

'God, there're times when I hate you.'

'No, you don't.' He grabbed her arm. 'You don't really, do you?' She looked down into his face. It was serious now. 'No. No, Jack, I don't.'

'Good. Then you can pour me another drop of wine, woman, before I go home. I can pick up the car tomorrow.' It was too soon to push things. Jack knew that, but given a little time, the situation might improve.

Rose changed her mind about painting a scene on Bodmin Moor. It still evoked too many bad memories. But she had decided to go further afield than West Cornwall to work.

Barry had taken her out for dinner, over which they had discussed some watercolours for a new batch of greetings cards he wanted her to do. It was too soon to start on them, they would have to wait for the spring when the pastels of hedgerow flowers would be at their best.

She sat, partly sheltered by rocks, and studied the bleak countryside around her. Ahead was the Cheesewring, a pile of large, smooth, flat stones balanced in such a precarious way it seemed they would fall over at the slightest touch. East Cornwall for a change, she had decided, with its varying shades of browns and greens although it was bleak in winter. She had gone for starkness again, which suited her style and the medium of oils. The Minnack work was finished, this would be the second in a series of six. Rose shivered. It was hard to believe what Geoff Carter had said. He had come to the house with a bottle of champagne and a broad smile on his face. 'Rose, you'll never guess,' he'd said. 'A gallery in Bristol wants to show twelve pieces of your work.'

Bristol. It wasn't London, but it was still an honour, and it would be the first time she had shown outside the county. She still couldn't believe her luck.

The wind was sharp and made strange noises amongst the stones but Rose was in her element. January was almost at an end. Her classes had resumed and it was still a pleasure to tutor Joel who continued to improve. He talked of Miranda who had settled down and found a job to keep her going until October.

Petra and Roger had telephoned. They had invited her

for dinner the following week. Rose sensed they would become close friends.

And there was Jack. She was seeing him tonight. They were going to the cinema then sharing a takeaway.

'The New Year's looking good,' she said as she angled her head to study the canvas. 'And so's this painting.'

Only when the cold began to seep into her bones did Rose pack up. She drove home and had a bath, sprayed her wrists with perfume and waited for Jack Pearce to come and collect her.